D1563496

God Forgives

The Streets Don't

Blake Karrington

Contents

Chapter 1	1
Chapter 2	14
Chapter 3	19
Chapter 4	28
Chapter 5	42
Chapter 6	56
Chapter 7	66
Chapter 8	74
Chapter 9	85
Chapter 10	95
Chapter 11	105
Chapter 12	119
Chapter 13	129
Chapter 14	140
Chapter 15	152
Chapter 17	176

Prologue

Watching him walk away through unblinking eyes, I was in pain like I had never suffered before. One thing was obvious, and that was the fact that even though I had taken numerous slugs, I was still alive. With that thought in mind, I knew that if I planned to stay alive, I needed to get help immediately.

Searching the parking lot for Monique, I thought it odd that after all the gunplay that had just taken place, she hadn't come to my assistance by now. Wondering what could have become of her, I began to drag my battered body towards my car, which at the moment, was the only thing I could think to do.

Oblivious to the stares of the slowly gathering crowd, I finally made it to the car and got inside after using every ounce of strength left in my steadily weakening body. Rummaging through my blood soaked pockets, I removed my keys and attempted to place them in the ignition as I recalled the parting words of my would-be assassin: I'll be sure to take care of your bitch!

Old thoughts of past friends and foes came to me as I lingered between coherence and oblivion. With every breath I took, another ghost from my past would glare at me in silent disgust. The faces of the many people who had shared my path through the years crowded my headspace. Their expressions clear against the backdrop of my blurry vision.

After all I'd lived through, all that I had accomplished; it seemed inconceivable that this was how it would end. Ironic, I guess, considering all of the death sentences I had handed down to unsuspecting lames for committing my exact offense. Getting caught slipping. The hunter had become the hunted.

This was the path that I had set for myself. What I did know, is that whatever my destiny called for, I would be prepared. When it was all said and done, what was life anyway? It was nothing more than a day to day struggle to survive. And no matter how much I wanted to walk away, there was no way that I could. I had been taught at an early age that "God forgives, the streets don't!"

Chapter 1

1991

Fresh out of jail for what I realized was more or less the fourth time, I found it hard to even enjoy the so called freedom I now had. Besides my new mentality, nothing in the free world had changed as far as I could tell. With no money, and the added responsibility of a new child on the way, I realized that the time for games had passed. Shit wasn't going to get better on its own, so I planned to force the hands of fate and come up by any means.

"It's cold out this bitch!" Sam snapped, rubbing his hands together and blowing out icy clouds of smoke. "Where the hell is this nigga at?"

Staring at his reflection in the freezing darkness, I wondered the same thing. Fingering the trigger of my .357 magnum, I gritted my teeth and chose not to give an answer to a question that neither of us could possibly know.

Feeling the vibration on my hip, I immediately forgot my previous thought and reached for the pager. Hitting the light in order to clearly see the number, I wasn't surprised to see my home number reflected back at me. The 911 code that preceded the number was only supposed to be used for emergencies. But when Monya called, in her mind, it was always an emergency.

See, Monya was my lady. She had held the title for the last seven years. Regardless of who I shared my time and body with, I had never loved another. At times like this, she had the ability to try my patience, but I guess that after seven consecutive years, it was nothing new.

Placing the pager back on my side, I surveyed the scene around me. With green fatigues on to match our beef and broccoli timbs, we fit in perfectly with the bushes we were entrenched in at the moment. The cold ground had the effect of making my freezing body ache. This also had the ability of making me angrier each minute I had to continue waiting for my unsuspecting victim.

Feeling the vibration again, I sucked my teeth in irritation. Already aware of who it was without even having to look, I reached down and turned it off. I was already aware that across the city, my baby was going to pitch a fit. But hey, if I didn't handle my business, we would never be able to experience any pleasure.

"Uhh!" Monya angrily exclaimed, tossing her arms up in a fed up manner. "I can't believe that motherfucker has the nerve to ignore my pages," she loudly snapped.

Pacing the floor, she couldn't help but envision numerous scenarios that would explain his not returning her calls. The one that came to mind was that Chez more than likely, was laid up somewhere with a trifling female.

At the thought alone, Monya began dialing his pager number again. Finding his pager cut off, only served to increase her rage.

Tired of his shit, she threw the phone against the wall with all her might. Folding her arms across her bosom, Monya made a silent promise to herself that as soon as she had the baby things were going to change in their relationship.

Glancing in the mirror, Monya saw her reflection staring back. Even with an angry scowl plastered over her features, she was a true beauty. She was a little heavier than she liked, due to the pregnancy, but she was beautiful, to say the least. Staring harder, Monya noted the long, lustrous, dark silky curls that framed her almond complexioned face. Her dark, smoldering eyes had an alluring presence that gave off an exotic quality. It was the beauty mole that sat right below her thick, succulent bottom lip, right between the point of her lip and chin, which certified her as a truly gorgeous creature.

As if seeing herself for the first time, Monya chewed on her bottom lip in silent contemplation. No longer angry, the thought surfaced that if she wanted, any nigga in the city would gladly fall at her feet. They never came outright with propositions, but their leering stares spoke their thoughts more clearly than any words ever could. Nevertheless, she wanted no one but Chez, and everyone knew it. Plus, his ass was known to act a fool, and niggas in the city were well aware that to mess with her was a guaranteed invitation for bloodshed.

Smirking, she poutingly stated, "You make me sick, nigga."

Running her manicured nails through her tresses, Monya plopped down on the foot of their bed. There was no getting around the fact that she was hopelessly in love. The worst part was, she had no control over her heart.

I was beginning to wonder if I'd been sent on a dummy mission as I looked at my watch. The nigga was over an hour late and I was freezing. After waiting in the cold all this time, I'd made up my mind that the bitch, Qwena, was wearing an ass whipping if her information turned out to be bogus.

Before I'd even finished having the thought, Sam signaled to let me know our vick had arrived. Turning in the direction of the loud music, I spotted the Cherokee and driver we'd awaited. The word on the wire was that he had cake. If that was the case, he would soon find out what happens when someone else wants your dough more than you. I was about to be on some pay me or pay the devil a visit shit real soon.

The Geto Boy's track, "My Mind Playing Tricks on Me," played at a deafening tone as he pulled into his driveway. Rico took his time exiting the vehicle. Slamming the door, he activated his key alarm before walking up the sidewalk with a shiny chrome 9 millimeter swinging by his side.

Watching from the shadows, it was amusing to me that his punk ass was trying to pimp as if he was tough. Signaling to Sam, I set the robbery in motion no sooner than Rico began to place his key in the door.

Turning his key, Rico heard footsteps approaching from behind. Alarmed, he attempted to turn in the direction of their approach. Before he could do so, a vicious blow to the back of his head from a heavy object, sent him reeling through the open door. Howling in pain, it took him a moment to register what had taken place.

Opening his eyes, Rico found himself staring down the barrel of a gun. I almost laughed out loud as Rico's eyes bulged when he saw me holding the gun. When he noticed Sam enter the house behind me, the look of terror on his face intensified. He seemed ready to vomit, shit himself, or both.

"I caught your ass slipping, didn't I, nigga?" I spat coldly.

Before Rico could respond, I said, "You know what it is. Now what's it gonna be, a robbery or a homicide?"

Thumbing back the hammer on the magnum, I patiently awaited Rico's answer.

We watched as his internal struggle played out in his features.

I bet that nigga is wondering how we found where he lays his head, I thought with a smirk. I could tell that his punk ass was afraid to die, and he already knew that I could pump him full of lead and go have a sandwich.

I wasn't surprised when he stammered "You can have it all, man."

Disgusted with Rico's weakness, I smacked him in the head with the pistol for the hell of it. In a flat, even tone, I said, "Lay all that shit out then, nigga. And just in case you try to play me, know that I'll gladly leave your ass leaking up in this bitch!"

"You don't have to hurt me, Chez. I'll get it, man."

Staring at him through beady eyes, I hissed, "Get my shit then, bitch!"

Holding his man down, Sam watched Rico like a hawk. One false move, and he would gladly let both barrels go on the sawed off. Known for having an itchy trigger finger, it wouldn't take much for that particular thought to become a reality. Sucking his teeth, he grinned at the sight before him.

I matched his grin, knowing that we were having the same thought. The nigga was just strolling cockily as if he had killer in his blood. Now, only minutes later, here he was crawling through the house on hands and knees with tears in his eyes.

Shaking his head, Sam mumbled, "The shit never fails."

Tired of dialing Chez's number, Monya curled up on the bed and hugged a pillow protectively. She felt so lost and alone. After all the years she and Chez had been together, it would seem that she would be accustomed to his disappearances, but that wasn't the case. When he wasn't in jail, which was seldom, he was still basically missing in action. Yet, she never strayed; always remaining faithful and trustworthy.

Monya could still recall the first time they met. He had been so handsome, in a rugged type of pretty boy way. His short, wavy hair, cinnamon complexion and hazel eyes were an immediate turn on for her. At 5 foot 9 he wasn't too tall, but his strength of character made him a prominent presence in her eyes.

Once they had become an item, Monya was in awe of the many stories he shared with her. From seeing his parents get murdered before his eyes, to growing up in countless foster homes, he'd experienced more than his share of suffering. These stories only served to solidify their relationship.

In Monya, Chez was able to find someone he could finally love and trust. Monya had found her soul mate in him, as well as someone who truly needed her.

Even now, when the road was somewhat rocky, she still felt that they shared their beginning bonds. Hopefully, when their child arrived, things would get better. Feeling the tears beginning to cloud her eyes, Monya sadly realized that they couldn't continue to live this way.

"Nigga, what the hell is this?" I angrily questioned. "Eight grand and three punk ass ounces. You have got to be kidding." Slapping

Rico in the face with the butt of my pistol, I snapped, "Where's the rest of it?"

Grabbing his badly bloodied face, Rico howled in pain. "I gave you everything I had, man. I swear to you, I wouldn't hold nothing back, Chez."

Pacing around the room, I had to take a moment to swallow his words. More than likely, he hadn't withheld anything, but in no way did that change the thoughts that now ran through my mind.

Catching Sam's eye, I silently conveyed my thoughts to my partner. Without having to say a word, Sam received the message that Rico was taking his last breaths at that very moment.

Breaking our stare, I swiveled to face Rico. Raising the Magnum, I began to speak in a slow, calculated tone. "Being that you only had eight grand and three ounces, I feel like you wasted my time. You already know I can't allow that, right?"

Throwing his hand's up in a futile attempt at blocking the shells that were now inevitable, Rico sobbed loudly. "Don't do this, man! Please don't do..."

Cutting his pleas short, I fired two well-placed slugs into Rico's throat. The force of the closely fired slugs severed the left side of his neck. With eyes that bulged out in shock, Rico wheezed loudly in an attempt to breathe. Squirming erratically in a quickly increasing pool of blood, he spewed a miniature blood fountain with each forced breath.

Having seen enough, I turned to walk away. Nodding my head in Rico's direction, I nonchalantly mumbled, "Finish him, bro."

Without hesitation, Sam walked over to Rico who was only seconds away from death, and let the sawed off roar. Without even giving him a second glance, Sam calmly strolled out the door. In his mind, it was all part of a day's work. Murder was never personal with him, bodying a nigga was strictly business.

Rolling through the strip, we puffed on a spliff of good green while acknowledging our people who held the block down by whatever means necessary. Raised within the same streets, I knew the rules and respected all those who played the game in the same manner as myself. Weak dudes were excluded; as an unwritten rule, if I was hungry they weren't allowed to eat. But in my hood, weak dudes weren't the norm. We prided ourselves on raising soldiers in the 3rd Ward, and that's just the way it was.

Whipping into the alley, my thoughts came to a halt. Before my eyes, the street opened into what resembled a block party. Wall to wall cars inched their way through the packed street. Ballers and the usual baller chasers were in attendance. A light sprinkling of junkies could be seen within the crowd, politicking in hopes of a quick hit or fix. Grinning inwardly, I exhaled a cloud of weed smoke as I pulled to the curb.

Handing the spliff to Sam, I said, "You ready, player?"

"You know I am," he exited the car to the sound of a female calling out to him.

Deciding that he would be held up for a while, I figured I'd go on without him and just catch up later. Making my way through the congested crowd, I was halted numerous times before reaching the spot. Between giving pounds to my homies and receiving numerous hugs from countless thick hoodrats, I thought I'd never make it through the door.

Once inside, I wasn't surprised to find that the crowd was standing room only. Nor was I surprised to see the crowd parting so that I could get through. Reaching the bar, I had to grin at the fact that in my city, I was the shit.

Turning around with two drinks in her hands, and her usual evil look in place, Kim laid eyes upon me. Her hard features immediately softened. Setting the drinks on the bar, Kim smiled. "Hey there, Chez. What you drinking tonight, baby?"

"What's up, boo? Give me a double gin and fix yourself something on me, alright?"

Winking her eye in a seductive fashion, she responded, "Your double gin's coming up. While I'm at it, I think I will take you up on that free drink."

Nodding my head in agreement, I sternly watched her walk away. Swiveling on the stool, I scanned the crowd to see if I could spot any of my crew in the place. Seeing no one, I heard Kim set my drink down on the bar behind me.

Turning back to face her, I took a sip from the drink, then asked, "Are any of my people in here, ma?"

"Umm Hmm. I haven't seen Dresser, but Boo-Boo and Satin are back there in the crap room."

Turning up my drink as I stepped off the stool, I said, "Thanks, ma." Flinging a 20 on the bar, I added, "Keep the change, and don't spend it all in one place either."

Smirking, I walked away, but not before her reply caught me.

"Pssst, big fucking spender!" Laughing, Kim loudly advised, "Don't get in no shit tonight either, nigga!"

Reaching the back room, Satin's voice was the first and loudest

I heard. Flanked by two dime pieces, he shook his hand feverishly, making the two dice he held tightly in his grasp clack audibly. Realizing that regardless of how loud they clacked, he had them locked. I awaited the set shot that all the silent onlookers were apparently dumb to.

"You niggas ready for this? Huh? Let me know something," he said, goading his opponents. Releasing the dice, he chuckled, "Seven, bitch!" Reaching around the board, Satin arrogantly stated, "That's right, pay me."

Shaking my head, it was funny to me how my dude had a knack for hustling hustlers and mackin' chicks. Even now, two women possessively held on to him as if he only belonged to them singularly. Without a doubt, Satin had to be the smoothest nigga I'd ever met, hands down. Locking eyes with Boo-Boo in the crowd, I started moving in his direction.

Boo-Boo and Satin were cousins. Like Satin, Boo-Boo also had game. The only difference between the two was Boo-Boo went hard. When shit got crazy, he was the one I wanted in my corner. While Satin was the player in their family, Boo-Boo was the gangster. It was a well-known fact throughout the city that when I went, he went; the other way around held just as true.

"What up, nigga? Where you been?" he questioned, never taking his eyes off Satin or the dudes crowded around him.

Following his eyes, I replied, "There was a little cash sitting in a motherfucker's safe that was in need of another home, so I had to make a run to pick it up."

Smirking, he cut his eyes in my direction. "Oh yeah? Why you ain't give me a holler, huh? It's like that now?"

"Nah, it ain't like that at all, Bro. Shit was sweet, and Sam was already with me, so there was no need to run around searching for you."

Narrowing his eyes, he spoke through clenched teeth. "Damn! You took that pretty nigga with you? You're lucky he didn't fuck around and get you killed."

Shrugging my shoulders carelessly, I ignored his comment, deciding to just let it go at that. Turning to scan the crowd and women in it, I thought to myself that there was definitely no love lost between the two of them. It was no mystery that Boo-Boo and Sam didn't get along.

As far as Boo-Boo's pretty boy comment, it only held true on the outside, because Sam had killer stamped all over his heart and mind. All who knew Sam, realized that the green eyed, light skinned nigga was far from soft. His hands and guns were official as they came.

"Yo, Boo-Boo, you seen any of my bitches up in here, man?"

"Yeah. The thick red bitch you bagged at Tracy's was up at the bar earlier. I know you're not tripping, but the nigga Herb was all up in her face on some fake mackin' shit."

"That nigga won't let a bitch live. If he don't do shit else, he will fuck something," I laughed, thinking that as long as it wasn't Monya that he was trying to get at, I couldn't care less.

As far as Missy was concerned, Herb hadn't done anything wrong. She was a bad bitch and he was supposed to try to get at her. Satin's voice interrupted my train of thought.

Flashing a large knot of bills, Satin boisterously stated, "I'm breaking these lames, bro. They don't have a clue, dog."

Extending my hand for our customary pound, I grinned. The grin wasn't so much for the words he had just spoken; it was due to the devious thoughts running through my mind. Even though I'd never play my man by trying to snag one of his women, I couldn't help the wicked thoughts I was having. If he offered, I'd gladly punish either one of the delicious looking females on his side.

Snapping out of my thoughts, I said, "We need to talk, bro."

"Not a problem, my nigga." Peeling bills from the knot he'd been flashing, Satin spoke in each of the female's ears before handing them the money and sending them on their way.

Turning back to face me, he said, "Okay what's on your mind, Chez?"

Taking a moment to formulate my words, I blurted out, "It's time to ante up and get this dough, player. Money is flowing through here like never before, and it's our time to come up in a major way, man."

"I'm already straight, bro. Right now, I can't see how shit could possibly get any better than this," he replied boisterously.

How did I know his petty ass would be on some 'I' shit? It always seemed to be strictly about Satin, and I was sick of it. Holding my rising temper in check, I decided to try a more diplomatic approach.

"Yeah, you're that nigga." I replied in a mocking tone. "Only thing is, why should you keep getting all these other niggas rich, copping weight for outrageous prices, when we can go up top and cop our own shit? Roll with me, nigga. I'm telling you, we can really blow."

Sighing, Satin looked everywhere but at me when he spoke. "You got a damn good idea, Chez, but I was always taught that if it ain't broke, don't fix it." Fidgeting, he threw it out there, "Let me stack some more dough, and in a couple months, we'll see, alright?"

"Yeah, Alright then," I answered, wanting to slap the shit out of his selfish ass.

I was willing to wait a couple months, but with or without him, it was going down. I was hungry, and if I had to die in order to reach my goals this time around, that was a price I was willing to pay.

Chapter 2

Covered in sweat, I released Missy's hips and watched as she sprawled flat out on her stomach. Even with her hair disheveled, she was a sight for sore eyes. Reaching for my boxers, I admired the back shot that was so inviting. Inviting or not, it was time to hit the road. The sun was my worst enemy, and the last thing I needed was for it to come up before I made it home.

Wiping a long wisp of hair out of her eyes, Missy looked over her shoulder and spoke in a sexy, teasing manner. "Where you going, Chez? We're not hardly finished yet, boo."

Grinning slyly, she turned on her side so that all her goodies were showcased properly.

Hesitating momentarily, my eyes were involuntarily glued to the delicious sight she presented, laying there looking like a video model. My bigger head won the battle, strengthening my resolve to get home to the video model that really counted. Shrugging my shoulders in a manner that basically said 'I'm sorry', I responded with five words that always had the ability to turn a female's smiles into frowns. "I gotta go home, ma."

Sucking her teeth loudly, Missy rolled her eyes, turned her back and buried her face in the pillow.

Making my way to the bathroom for a well needed shower, I thought, oh well, if she didn't know by now, she should have. No woman came before, Monya. Whether she chose to respect it or not, was her option. But like all the rest, I had no doubt that she would play the game by my rules.

Arriving at home, I glanced upward. I'd beat the sun this time, but the burnt orange texture of its appearance was slowly creeping through the darkness of night as I exited the car. Strolling towards the house, I was sure that Monya would be wide awake and in wait of my entrance. Placing my key in the door, I prepared myself for the argument that I knew was coming.

Opening the door, I sighed slightly at the sight of Monya's silhouette sitting motionless on the couch, in the dark. "Hey baby. What you doing sitting in the dark?"

"Hey baby, my ass!" she snapped, jumping up from the couch. "Where the fuck have you been, Chez? Why the hell is your pager turned off?" she blurted out angrily, pointing her finger accusingly.

Cutting my eyes evilly at the finger that was only inches from my face, I concluded that her argument would fade if I ignored her. Tossing my keys on the counter, I walked past her as if she wasn't even standing there.

"Nigga, don't ignore me!" she ranted, stalking my every step.

Reaching the bedroom, I perched on the edge of the bed and began to remove my boots. Tuning out her angry taunts, I tossed them in the closet. With her damn near standing between my legs, removing my socks and fatigues was awkward, but not impossible.

"I'm sick of your shit, Chez! Either you get it together or I swear that when I have this baby, I'm leaving your ass," she threatened with a quivering voice and tear filled eyes.

Glancing up into her face with an incredulous look, I dropped the shirt I'd just pulled over my head. No longer able to ignore her, Monya had garnered my complete attention with her matter of fact statement.

"Huh?" I asked dumbfounded. With a stone face, I mumbled, "What did you just say, Monya?"

Subtly taking a step backwards, Monya hesitantly stated, "You heard me. I said you have to—"

Allowing my eyes to appraise my woman, I refused to even entertain the thought of her going anywhere. Leave me. Psst, never! Not in a million years would I allow that. In a zone, I took notice of the way her thick nipples pushed at the fabric of her short-shirt. Even pregnant, Monya was beautiful. Short and thick, Monya was blessed with the exotic features of a China doll. Dark, sexy eyes, cold black, long silky hair and thick, juicy thighs that connected to an award winning ass were just a few of the physical features that held my attention through the years. Even now, as I watched her mouth moving, I realized that I had to have her. Reaching outwards, I grabbed two hands full of ass and pulled her to me.

Gently biting her nipple through the thin shirt, I ignored her weak struggles. Palming her ass, I squeezed the cheeks tightly, while sucking as much of her breast into my mouth as possible. Feeling her fingers begin to roam through my hair, along with her quickened breaths, I knew we were on the same page.

Releasing my hold, I held her gaze as I removed my boxers then her shirt. With nothing on but panties, I slowly placed my thumbs in the band on both sides and began to lower them. Locking her dreamy eyes on the dick, she slowly raised one leg then the other, before stepping completely out of them.

Wrapping her hair in my hands, I pulled her body down flat on my own as our lips locked in a silent, hungry battle. Adjusting her frame further down on my torso, I felt her lips engulf the head of my dick. Unable to contain my lust, I raised my hips off the bed and buried my swollen head inside her warm tight, satiny soft insides.

"Umm" Monya groaned at the feel of the sweet invasion. Breaking the kiss, but holding eye contact, she slowly began to rotate her hips in an attempt to take as much of me inside her as possible.

Gripping Monya's ass to control the depths of my thrust, I stared into the bottomless pools of her dark eyes. I could honestly say that she was the only woman I ever loved, and at times like this, I couldn't quite understand why I gave myself to any other besides her.

Arching her back, Monya got all the way into the ride she was experiencing. "Mmm, Chez. You... feel...so...good...baby!" she whimpered, bucking up and down on the dick with her head thrown back in ecstasy.

Meeting her stroke for stroke, I held her swollen, jiggling breast with the nipples trapped tightly between my index and middle fingers. Feeling her pace quicken, it was evident due to her moans and the loud slapping sounds her ass was making every time it connected with my thighs, her climax was rapidly approaching.

"Chez, Chez. Oh, shit! Damn, Baby!" Monya whimpered, leaning back to grasp my thighs with her eyes clamped tightly.

Trembling, on the brink of cumming myself, I sadly experienced a twinge of jealousy at the thought of my boo riding another nigga like this. Umph umm! I wasn't hardly gonna allow that to happen. Right then, I decided that from this moment on, it was strictly gonna be about Monya and our child. There would be no more bullshitting in the streets with loose, gold digging females. Feeling Monya's juices pouring over me with her pulsating climax, I closed my eyes to the realization that although I meant what I was saying, a new day was arriving with the coming sun. The only question that ran through my mind as I shot my second load of the night into my baby was how would I feel when the new day arrived?

Chapter 3

Awakening, I rolled over and glared through slits at the clock that sat on the dresser. Needing to get out of bed, I couldn't seem to make my body work along with my mind. Although the clock read 1:40 PM, after murdering a nigga, sexing two women back to back, and not getting to sleep until the break of day, I was truly exhausted.

Exhaling, it was apparent that I had too many tasks that needed to be attended to, so I removed the covers and sleepily sat up in bed. Reaching for my cigarettes and vibrating pager in the same motion, I squinted my eyes to see who was blowing me up. Frowning at the number that continuously popped up on the screen, I tossed the pager back on the night stand with no intention of returning the call.

Sparking the Newport, I had to shake my head at the thought of Qwena's worrisome ass sweating a nigga all early and shit. After giving up the whereabouts of Rico's crib, she was ready to get broke off. Oh, well. As far as I was concerned, the nigga never came home. Releasing a cloud of smoke, I grinned at the thought of her never receiving a dime of my blood money. Fuck her! She wasn't new to the game, so her trifling ass shouldn't have a problem with taking the loss.

Puffing on my first Backwood of the day, I whipped through the city as if the streets belonged to me. Reaching over to raise the volume on the stereo, I leaned further back in the seat as the euphoric feeling of the weed seemed to suddenly take effect. Other than the fact that I had no license, I was actually feeling pretty good. Between the money that was weighing down my pockets, and the plans I had to flip it into a dynasty, I couldn't see how anything could spoil my mood.

On that note, I figured that maybe it would be sensible to grab myself a driver so that I could ride trouble free. Dresser was the first face that popped into my mind; the only thing he loved more than looking fly, was driving. Immediately changing my route, my new destination was Dresser's crib.

Arriving at his house, I hit the horn. Seeing the door open, I wasn't surprised when Monica's nosey ass stepped outside in a pair of shorts that emphasized her every curve. Gawking openly at the sight before me, I couldn't help admiring how finely she was put together. Monica was a true cutie and she damn well knew it.

Sashaying to the car, she seductively ran her tongue over glossed lips, before saying, "What's going on, Chez?"

Smiling at her obvious flirting, I replied, "You know me, shawty." And she did, because before my man came along, I had hit it a few times myself. "Where's my man, ma?"

Frowning at the mention of Dresser, Monica replied, "You already know he's in there doing his usual. Nothing."

Laughing at her reply, I couldn't help thinking that the disrespectful bitch was too much for my man. In my opinion, she was in need of some raw discipline, but control was something he was definitely lacking when it came to women.

Prancing back towards the house, she smiled before asking, "You coming in or do you plan to keep staring at my ass?"

Caught, I got out the car and followed her inside. Trying to ignore her body, I found the task entirely too hard to even bother. Our close proximity made it impossible not to scrutinize the jiggle that was taking place beneath her thin, cotton shorts. Shaking my head, I had to snap out of the trance her ass had placed upon me.

Entering the den, I spotted Dresser watching television. Giving him a pound, I said, "What you planning to do today, my man?"

"I ain't doing shit. Why? What's up?" he questioned with little enthusiasm.

Taking a second to scan his attire, it seemed odd to me that the nigga wore every piece of jewelry he owned. He was dressed fly enough for a night out at an exclusive club and didn't have any plans besides watching television.

Snapping out of my thoughts, I said, "You trying to roll with me?"

The questioning look I saw him toss in Monica's direction had me puzzled. It seemed as if he actually needed her to make the decision for him. Staring from one to the other, I disgustedly waited to see just how the situation would play out.

Popping her lips, Monica rolled her eyes, "Hell yeah, he's trying to roll with you. Take him on a stick-up or something before you bring him back too. We need some money up in this bitch!" She mumbled, "He needs to do something instead of sitting up in my face all day," as she strutted out the room.

Wishing that he would slap the shit out of her, I watched his shoulders slump in defeat as he turned to me and stated, "I'm rolling with you, dog."

Smiling sarcastically, I said, "It pretty much seems that way. Now don't it?"

Riding through the hood, I spotted Sam in an alleyway holding one of his pits. Pointing towards him, I said, "Pull over there, Dresser."

Glancing at our approach, the gathered crowd went back to doing what they were involved in when they saw that it was only us. Coming to a stop near the alley, I rolled the window down and called out to Sam, "Yo, come take a ride with me, Bro."

Handing the chain and dog to one of the homies, Sam jumped in. Inhaling the aroma, he reached for the Backwood.

"What's up with you, nigga?" he asked, before leaning back and drawing on the weed.

"You're what's up, my nigga," was my reply as I tossed an ounce and two grand in the back seat. "Yo, Kid, you already know we came up on some short shit last night, so I'm gonna have to make your cut up later. I got to make some major moves with the rest of the loot, cuz. You already know I got you when shit gets straight, alright?"

"Man, you already know I ain't trippin'." Counting the money, he said, "Here, Bro, flip this ounce with the rest of what you got."

Reaching over the seat, I gave him a pound. "That's what's up, dog. You can believe me when I tell you, we're gonna come up big off this little shit. I'm telling you both, this is it."

"Yeah, yeah. I believe you, nigga. Now take me back around the way. I got shit to do," Sam laughed.

Grinning at what Sam said, I was just imagining what my niggas would be saying when my plans were no longer plans, but our everyday reality. When it was all said and done, I'd make believers out of everyone.

After dropping Sam off, we decided to hit the mall. I wanted to buy something nice for Monya. She deserved it, and I figured a gift would help to smooth over any irregular thoughts she may have been harboring behind last night.

Strolling through the crowded mall, I was treated to a buffet of some of the baddest females in the city. Some I knew, and the rest were prospects that I would have liked to get to know. That is, if I hadn't made the promise to myself that I was going to refrain from messing around with other chicks.

Taking a deep breath, I made an unspoken oath to stay focused. I continued walking, ignoring the flirtatious stares that were being thrown my way, from every direction. Heading into Victoria Secret, my steps were halted at the sound of someone loudly calling my name. Turning around, I came face to face with the last person I'd expected to encounter.

"You can't return my calls no more, nigga?" Qwena loudly questioned in a stink voice. Ready to cause a scene, she began to point her index finger as if it were a gun. "Let me tell your red ass something..."

"You're just the bitch I've been looking for!" I snapped, cutting her words short as I turned the tables on her. Moving with the speed of light, I glared viciously as I grabbed her throat. Wanting to laugh at the fear that was suddenly evident in her wide eyes, I hissed, "What kind of games you trying to play with that bogus ass information you gave me? Do you take me for a motherfucking chump or something, shawty?"

Nervously blinking, she began to stutter, "Uh, what...you... talking...about...baby?" Lowering her voice, Qwena apologetically stated, "I'd never try to play you, boo. Believe me."

Mean mugging, I inwardly grinned at the picture she presented.

No longer loud or arrogant, she was soaking up my act like a sponge. Catching the eyes of her assembled entourage, it was apparent that they too were buying my show of anger by the way they averted their eyes when I glared in their direction.

"Look. Don't ever pull any shit like that again. You hear me?" I menacingly stated.

"I won't," she responded agreeably. With downcast eyes, she said, "I could have sworn I gave you the right address though. Plus, I've been calling him all day and he hasn't returned my messages yet. That's why I figured you got to him, boo."

Averting my eyes at her truthful words, it was hard to keep a straight face. "Nope, he never came to where I was. I missed him this time. But for future reference, I'd suggest that the next time you feel like stepping to me with some bullshit, you miss me as well," I spat, releasing my hold on her throat.

Before she could reply, Dresser gave me the exit I'd been searching for. "Let's roll, Bro. You know we got shit to take care of."

Acknowledging his statement with a nod, I said, "I'll holler at you, ma."

Turning to walk away, I felt a light tug on my jacket. Thinking, what now? I glanced behind me to find Qwena staring expectantly at me.

"Can I see you later, Chez?" Locking eyes with me, she ran her tongue over a pair of the loveliest full lips ever. "I promise to make it worth your while."

Weakening rapidly, I found it impossible to ignore the gesture she made with her tongue. Not to mention the fact that her promise of making it worth my while had been proven on too many occasions for tonight to be an exception. So much for my oath of monogamy. I was hitting her sexy ass before the night was over and it hadn't even been twenty-four hours since I made my vow.

"Yeah. I think we may just be able to link up, ma. I'll call you with the time later, alright?"

Grinning, she enthusiastically stated, "I'll be awaiting your call, baby."

Walking off, I noticed the smirk that was plastered upon Dresser's face.

Smiling myself, I inquired, "What? Why you looking like that, dog?"

Shaking his head, Dresser replied, "You never cease to amaze me man. Regardless of how badly you treat these silly bitches, they still be sweating you."

Shrugging my shoulders, I couldn't argue with the truth. Some of us have the gift, and others don't. I was just blessed with the ability to control females, without giving them the ground that I knew they would use to turn the tables on me, if given the chance. As far as I was concerned, you either ran the show or got run over. Living by that rule, I refused to falter in my game, regardless of who liked it.

After dropping Dresser off, I wasn't trying to bump into the boys in blue, so I stuck to the back streets and made sure to duck all drug zones on the way home.

Bopping my head to the sounds pouring through the system, I was interrupted by the vibration I felt on my hip. Unsnapping the miniature box from my side, I was presented with a familiar number. Before I could replace it, the vibration began again. Glancing back at the screen, I wasn't surprised to see that it was Monya again. Tossing the pager on the passenger seat, it dawned on me that this same scene had been played out in the exact manner months before. Drifting back in time, I found myself reflecting upon the events of that seemingly long ago day.

5 months prior

Tossing the pager on the passenger seat, I exhaled in an attempt to calm the building irritation I experienced each time Monya paged me. Knowing I needed to call her back, I decided instead to wait until I got home. I was almost there already, so what difference would a few more minutes make?

Entering our neighborhood, I couldn't quite figure out what it was, but something just didn't feel right. It was as like an eerie feeling of lurking doom somewhere up ahead. Ignoring the signs, I pulled in front of our house and exited the whip in a hurry. Before I'd taken a dozen steps, it seemed as if the entire street had broken out in chaos. Men ran at me from every direction, screaming orders, with weapons drawn. Caught off guard, I could do nothing but sprawl out on the ground, place my hands behind my head, and angrily glaring at the horde of U.S. Marshals and A.T.F. agents that surrounded me.

I was immediately extradited back to Maryland, where I was arraigned on charges stemming from a case I'd caught a year earlier. From the way it looked, the feds were planning to make me sorry for ever carrying the Mac 11 nine millimeter with infrared scope and 500 rounds of ammo up the highway. Things were definitely looking dire, and without a bond, Baltimore jail had become my home. The mice and rats that ran rampant through its halls were the family I'd been given.

Down and out, with little to no hope for a change in my new reality, I was granted a gift from God. After four and a half months, my case was dropped due to a technicality. Unbelievably, I was free to pick up where I'd left off. After facing a lengthy stay in the federal penitentiary, I'd been granted a reprieve. After what I'd experienced, I made up my mind that the time had come to get what was owed to me in the game. The new me had been born, and it was on...

Snapping out of my reflection as I pulled on my street, I noticed that unlike the day in my thoughts, everyone was out and about. Before the car had even come to a complete stop, Monya opened the door and stepped outside. No longer irritated with her blowing up my pager, it suddenly dawned on me that the woman before me had been through pure hell with me through the years, while a lesser woman would have bailed on her man long ago.

Reaching for her gift in the passenger seat, I stepped from the vehicle. Seeing the slight smile that replaced the frown once embedded in her features, as she glanced from the Victoria Secret bag back to my face, I slowly cracked a smile as well.

Holding her lingering gaze, I hoped that she would never lose the faith that she held in me; it was warranted this time. With the six grand and three ounces in my possession, I was about to take our standard of living to an elevated level. As if awakening all over again, I needed no clock this time to inform me that I had much that needed my attention. It was written in stone, so I would tackle the come-up task with an intensity that was inhuman until I reached my goal.

Chapter 4

The block was booming as usual. In fact, it was on fire. Between trying to serve constant unrelenting traffic, and looking over my shoulder for the roving police patrols, I was just as tired as any 9 to 5 worker on an honest grind. Only unlike them, the money that weighed heavily in each of my pockets gave me the added incentive to put in overtime.

The last few months I'd spent on the block going hand to hand, was somewhat new to me. My hustle up to this point had relied strictly upon sticking up, with a contract murder or two on the side from time to time. Yet, my change of career turned out to be even more lucrative than I'd expected. In a relatively short period of time, I'd become the man with the hook-up. All the fiends were searching for my sack and I was trying to be found.

"You good?" I asked placing twenty-five, five dollar bags in the hand of a fidgety smoker in exchange for a crispy hundred dollar bill.

"Umm hmm. Thanks Chez.," she tossed over her shoulder, scurrying off without even glancing back.

Shaking my head in her wake, I reached in the big bag to handle my next sale. It was then that I heard a familiar voice behind me.

"What can I get for nothing, nigga?" Boo-Boo taunted.

Turning to the voice, I gave my nigga a pound. Sending the pipehead on his way, I grinned. "Where you been hiding at, Bro? A nigga ain't seen you in a minute."

Sparking a blunt that smelled like something else may have been sprinkled inside, he replied. "You know me, player. I'm always on the creep one way or another. But enough about me, what's been going on with you?" Waving his arms around, he grinned, "They tell me, you got the block on fire these days."

Raising my brow in dismay, I humbly stated, "Who, me? They must have meant another Chez."

"Imagine that," he chuckled. Pausing to let the next customer receive his issue, Boo-Boo said, "Seriously though, you're doing your thing nigga. I'm feeling that."

Pocketing the money from my last sale, I said, "Shit's moving around here for real, dog. At this rate, it won't be long at all til I'll have my weight up." Reaching inside the bag to serve the next customer in line, I added, "You know how it is, cuz."

Cutting his eyes at the constantly approaching traffic, he asked, "What the hell you got in those bags, nigga? These motherfuckers ain't stopped coming since I got here and Satin's spot looks like a ghost town."

"I got that fire, nigga! Nah. On the real, I took a gamble and tried something new. I came out with five dollar joints, while everyone else is competing with ten dollar bags. The shit actually worked, man. They love it, and this is the easiest money I've ever made without a gun."

Clearly impressed, Boo-Boo questioned, "Five dollar bags, huh? Damn! How the hell do you make money giving the shit away?"

"That's how I make money, my man. Just like you, everyone thinks I'm giving the shit away. Only, what they don't realize is, I'm seeing a profit of twelve hundred quick dollars off every ounce I flip, while Satin and the rest of them are left holding their shit."

Shaking his head in understanding, Boo-Boo agreed, "You're right, kid. You definitely seem to have started something special around here. Get your money, my nigga."

"I'm gonna try my best. You can believe that." I stated more serious than he could have ever imagined.

"Yo, I gotta go, Bro. But what you think about us heading to the club tonight, being that we haven't hung out in a while?"

Figuring that I'd been putting in a lot of time on the block without any real fun time on the side, I couldn't see why a night on the town wouldn't be justified. "Yeah, man, we can do that. I need a break anyway."

"That's what's up then. I'll let the rest of the crew know, and give you a call later," he added, walking up the block.

Thinking about the night ahead of me, I went back to serving the fiends that surrounded me. I was in no way blind to the fact that although everything was going well at the moment, the other dealers would catch on to my scheme sooner or later. Stacking dough was my way of beating out the competition I would be faced with when that time arrived. Therefore, all I had on my mind was hustling hard to achieve my goal of going to New York where I could step my position of power up another level. Smiling inside, I knew that at the rate I was moving, it wouldn't be much longer before I was ready to make my move.

Finding Monya to be unusually quiet when I arrived home, I chalked it up to nothing more than another pregnant mood swing.

After showering and getting dressed, I expected her to raise hell in an attempt to keep me home, but all I found was her in bed with a solemn look upon her face. Wondering what could be wrong, I took a seat on the side of our bed and rubbed her silky hair. "You alright, baby?"

"Umm hmm. I'm fine," she replied in a hoarse sort of way.

Leaning forward, I placed a gentle kiss on her lips. "You sure, boo? I can stay home if something's wrong."

"No. You go ahead and enjoy yourself, baby. I'll be just fine," Monya said, clenching the sheets tightly as another sharp pain shot through her middle.

Rising from my sitting position, I couldn't put my finger on it, but I knew that something wasn't right. However, since she willingly gave me the green light, I wasn't going to argue with her.

Grabbing my gun and keys, I kissed her again. "Don't wait up for me, baby. I'll more than likely be out real late, alright?"

She shook her head in understanding. Her expression telling me to shut up and leave before she changed her mind

Exiting the house, my mind was on my scheduled rendezvous with my crew that I was running late for. Little did I know, if I would have turned back around instead of rushing from the house, I could have been by Monya's side when she went into labor. By the time I laid eyes on my woman again, I would be seeing her along with my newborn baby girl.

Arriving in the city, I couldn't wait to reach the club and indulge in all the happenings that I knew awaited. I loved to party in the city. The main reason I enjoyed myself here was that the dudes in the

city carried it just like I did, while others carried it like I planned to. Between the increased murder rate and the high powered flossing, Richmond was renowned all over the country.

Pointing up ahead, Dresser turned the music down a couple decibels. "Ain't that Paulette and them, Bro?"

Broad Street was packed, making it hard for me to immediately see them in the crowd, but I saw where they were parked when Satin pulled to the curb beside them. Locking my eyes on one of them in particular, I answered, "Yeah, that's them."

Excitedly, Dresser exclaimed, "I'm trying to holler at Paulette. Pull over there, nigga."

I had already planned to roll up on them for my own reasons, before he suggested doing so. Locking eyes with my prey, I parked behind Satin's whip. Stepping from the car, I openly stared at Neeta. The slight smile that lit up her face let me know that she was aware of what I wanted.

Now the only problem was Sam, posted up in her face. He was my nigga and the last thing I wanted to do was carry it foul behind a female, but I'd had my eyes on her for the longest time. I planned to have her for myself and that was all there was to it.

"Hey Chez."

Breaking my eye contact with Neeta, I turned to acknowledge the sexy voice that had spoken my name. Seeing Sonya, Tasha and Paulette standing with Satin, Boo-Boo and Dresser, I nodded my head in their direction.

Turning back to Neeta, I muscled in on the conversation she shared with Sam. "What's up with you, shawty?"

Having an unmistakable meaning behind my words, Neeta

blushed sexily. Widening her already beautiful smile, she laughed, "Ain't nothing going on with me, Chez. How about yourself?"

Ignoring the stares of everyone around us, I licked my gold suggestively. "The only thing of interest as far as I'm concerned is the way you're wearing the hell out that catsuit." Scanning her frame from head to toe, I flirtatiously added, "You're wearing that shit real well too, ma."

At a loss for words, she stared in open mouthed amusement, shaking her head.

Laughing, Satin cut in, "Come on, nigga. We have a club to go to, so there's no need for us to stay out here."

In agreement, I winked my eye at Neeta and turned to walk away. From the corner of my eye, I peeped Sam staring evilly in my direction.

Without another thought to him or what may have been on his mind, I tossed the words, "I got your drinks when we get inside, ma," over my shoulder.

I was getting her, and hopefully he would understand that this was bigger than him.

Monya was in a cold sweat as Yaya gripped her hand. "Breathe girl. It's gonna be alright," she consoled with tears in her eyes to match the ones in her best friend's.

"It hurts," Monya gasped in pain. "I didn't know it was going to hurt this bad, Yaya. Shit!" she wailed.

Wondering why Chez hadn't called back, Yaya nervously watched the phone, thinking that it was fucked up that her girl was suffering while he was out doing God knows what. She heard Monya call her name.

"Yaya…ahhh! Yaya, call Chez again…please!" Whimpering, Monya clamped her eyes tightly together. Under her breath, she prayed, "Please God, don't let me have to suffer through this alone. Where are you, Chez?"

Bypassing the long line, we were able to walk straight in the club. Boo-Boo knew the girl on the door, so a hundred dollars and a kind word opened the entrance to Ivory's and all the thick dimepieces that awaited us.

Checking out the scantily dressed cuties that seemed to be everywhere, we made our way through the crowd. Reaching the bar, I grabbed a bottle of Moet. It wasn't necessarily my drink of choice, but the bottle itself was an attention grabber and if you claimed to be ballin', it was a must.

Turning the bottle up, I caught sight of one of my mans. Heading in his direction, I saw that his whole crew was in attendance. Grabbing his shoulder, I said, "I see all the ballers are out tonight."

Spinning around to see who had their hand on him, Scooter had a mean mug in place. Seeing me changed the mug to a grin. "Damn! What's up, nigga?" Giving me a hug, he said, "I heard you got fucked up with the feds, man."

"Yeah. They had a nigga, but I'm good now, though," I grinned.

Seeing the way the diamonds were glittering in his medallion, I decided that he was a whole lot better. Unable to hold my thoughts, I stated, "From the looks of it, you and your people are doing the motherfucker!"

"Nah," he laughed, taking a sip of some kind of exotic blue concoction. "We're not like that, Bro."

"Yeah. Whatever, nigga!" Playfully reaching for his chain as I glanced down at my own, I said, "Diamonds don't lie, kid."

Scooter and the Fulton Hill members that were in earshot of my comment shared a laugh.

Laughing as well, I caught the eye of a pretty, chocolate stunner. Raising the bottle of Moet to my lips, I gave her an appreciative glance as she raised her finger, motioning me to the dance floor. Setting my bottle on the table, I strolled out on the floor where she was already gyrating seductively to the music.

Melding my body to hers, we immediately began to wine to the thunderous reggae sounds. With each boom from the speakers, her swirling hips sent an intense vibration through my center. Pressing back with the same urgency, I realized that this was exactly why I had come here. It suddenly became obvious as I watched her phat, soft ass bounce up against me that I wouldn't be leaving alone.

Grabbing her arm as the second song ended, I gently pulled her towards the bar and the privacy it offered us. Reaching the bar, I turned to her. "Who are you, and what are you drinking?" I questioned.

Speaking in a raspy tone, she replied, "I'm Mia, and I'm drinking the same thing you were drinking when you saw me."

Giving her a lustful look, I noticed the way she returned my look with the same unblinking stare. The way she bit her lip, as if she was in deep thought, was so sexy to me. "I'll take a bottle of Moet for the lady," I informed the bartender, reaching for my roll of money to pay the tab.

"Nah, love. I got this," she said, reaching past me with a Benjamin.

Her free hand rested on the hand I had stuffed inside my pants pocket.

"Oh, yeah," I thought, liking her style already. Mia was my type, and I planned to get to know her a whole lot better before the night ended.

Handing her the bottle, I leaned against the bar and gave her the once over appraisal. Getting straight to the point as I watched her wrap her glossy lips around the bottle, I asked, "What are your plans for the rest of the night, Mia? I have none, so I'm looking for something to get into."

Releasing her lip lock on the bottle with a light sucking sound, she leaned towards me. "My plans are your plans, cutie. We're connected for the night as far as I'm concerned," she stated matter-of-factly.

Feeling her style, I thought to myself that she had a way with words that rivaled my own. "We can definitely stick together tonight, ma. I was hoping you would feel that way, for real."

"I'm ready for that drink, Chez," Neeta spat with attitude.

Hearing what sounded like a demand, I turned around to see what resembled a jealous look plastered across her irritated features. Smiling, it struck me that she was beautiful, even when she was angry.

Rolling her eyes to the ceiling, Neeta snapped, "You said you would have me something to drink when we got inside. Now I want it," she said, cutting her eyes defiantly in Mia's direction.

Enjoying her little show of aggression, I figured I'd play with her a little longer before buying the drink. Placing my arms around Mia's waist, I smiled, "Oh, where's my manners. Neeta, I'd like you to meet Mia. Mia, meet Neeta…"

36

Cutting the introductions short, Neeta sucked her teeth. "Whatever, nigga! I'm ready for my drink, Chez." Placing her hands on her hips, she waited.

Smiling inwardly, I turned to Mia. "Give me a moment to handle this, and we can pick back up where we left off, alright?"

Folding her arms over a pair of ample breasts, she smiled. "I'm not going anywhere, handsome. Go ahead and handle your business," she said, sneering antagonistically in Neeta's face. Lifting the bottle of Moet up in a mock sort of toast, she winked her eye before seductively whispering, "Don't make mama wait too long, baby."

Exhaling at the unspoken implications of her last statement, I followed Neeta to the far corner of the bar. Although I had a sure thing for tonight with Mia, that in no way stopped me from going straight at Neeta no sooner than we were out of earshot.

Leaning against Neeta as she stood in front of me at the bar, I felt her every curve as I pressed my body firmly against her back. "Hey, beautiful."

"Hey nothing," she snapped, pushing her body more firmly against mine. Ordering her drink, she turned her head to face me. "You could have done better for yourself than that hoodrat back there, Chez."

Removing a fifty dollar bill from my pocket, I grinned. "You think so, huh?"

Sucking her teeth, she snapped, "Hell yeah, you could!"

Running my palms from her small breast across her flat stomach, to her thick thighs, I replied, "I'd rather be with you."

Staring over her shoulder, she said, "You would, huh?"

Holding eye contact, I blurted out, "You damn right I would!"

We'd already been served our drinks, but we still continued to hold our position at the bar. With my dick pressed comfortably between the crease of her ass, I grabbed a napkin and pencil from the bar and wrote my number down. Placing the number in her palm, I said, "Give me a call, ma. From there, we'll just see where we end up, alright?"

Folding her hand around the napkin, Neeta grabbed her drink and said, "We'll have to see about that."

Nibbling on her ear, I said, "We'll just have to see then, won't we?"

Walking away, I knew that she would call me sooner or later, so it was time to seal the deal with Mia.

Engrossed in the music, Mia jumped when I whispered in her ear. "Come on, ma. We need to go somewhere more secluded and get properly acquainted."

Grabbing my hand, she replied, "Let's go, mind reader."

Making our way through the crowd, I spotted my crew and headed in their direction. Neeta stood nearby with her girls, so she was able to hear me when I said, "I'll get up with you niggas, tomorrow."

Throwing my keys to Dresser, I loudly added, "I have a ride, so I won't be needing those tonight."

Pulling Mia by the hand, I noticed the appreciative glances my partners were giving her as we walked off. Unable to resist a sideways glance at Neeta on the way past, it was clear that she didn't like the plans I'd made for the evening, or the person I'd made them with.

Winking my eye, I blew her a goodnight kiss.

I could feel Neeta staring daggers into my back as I made my way to the exit with Mia. I knew that she was cussing me out in her mind, but I also knew that she would be calling soon.

After riding in the new 5 series BMW that sported rims more expensive than the average nigga's whole whip, I wasn't surprised when we reached her apartment. Located in one of the most exclusive neighborhoods in the city, her crib was lavish as hell. Looking around, it was clear that someone had dropped major dough decorating the apartment in the splendor that was showcased around me. Seeing her remove her heels, I followed suit. Removing my own shoes, the plushness of the thick, soft carpet felt good.

"You thirsty, cutie?" Mia questioned, removing her skirt as if it were a normal occurrence.

Watching her strut towards the kitchen on the next level, I licked my lips at the sight of all that ass pouring out of French cut, lace panties. Clearing my throat, I said, "I'll take some orange juice if you have some."

Catching me staring as she looked back, Mia giggled, "I got you, boo."

That was one thing she didn't have to sell me on. I knew she had me in more ways than one. As fine as she was, she needed to know that I had her too, I thought, getting more comfortable in the loveseat.

Hearing her coming, I opened my eyes to a sight that pleasantly surprised me. No longer wearing anything but her jewelry, Mia draped her chocolate frame across my lap and began feeding me the orange juice. Removing the glass from my lips, she replaced it with her own. Tracing the contours of my lips with her tongue, our kiss intensified to the point where I somehow ended up naked with her straddling my lap.

Breathing rapidly, Mia slid from my lap to the floor. Looking up into my eyes with her own lust-filled eyes, she instructed, "Open your legs, boo."

Doing as she had instructed, I opened them wide and stared down into Mia's lingering gaze. Never losing eye contact, I watched her slowly move her juicy lips down my rock hard dick. I couldn't believe my eyes or ears for that matter, when I watched every single inch disappear down her throat to the loud moans that I was shocked to find out where my own.

Weak and too hoarse to scream, Monya laid in bed soaking wet. Pushing with every ounce of strength she had left, her grunts and whimpers sounded like those of a wounded animal.

Sweaty and tired as well, Yaya held her girl's hand, instructing over and over, "Push, Monya! She's almost out, girl! Come on now. You can do it, girl."

Working feverishly between her wide open thighs, the doctor calmly stated, "Here she comes, Monya. That's right. Push harder."

Tossing her head from side to side like a mad woman, Monya growled as she pushed with all her might. After being in labor for hours, she suddenly felt the baby she'd been carrying for 9 months come out. "Finally," she thought, unable to even force a smile from her cracked, parched lips.

Hearing the smack and instant wail of her healthy daughter, Monya bit her tongue in disgust. She was proud to have become a mother, but disgusted that her baby's father had been a no-show at the time when she needed him most. Closing her eyes, Monya decided that like every other mistake Chez had made, she would forgive him. The only difference was, this time his strike had hurt her so badly that she would never forget it. Seeing the sun shining through the window, the only question she had was, where is he?

Chapter 5

1992

With the New Year behind me, business on the strip had picked up drastically. The only problem was, along with the New Year came a major drought. Suddenly, I could hardly find the product needed to maintain the block. All over the city, dealers were experiencing the same problem that plagued me. Not only was the situation hectic, but when product was available, the prices were ridiculously high. Damn near feeling as if I were being robbed, I was tempted to unveil my pistols and get it how I live.

Thanks to Boo-Boo and his vast connections throughout Richmond, I was able to score whatever I needed while the rest of the dealers in the city suffered. He had come through for me in my time of need, and the rapidly diminishing space within my safe was proof of what those connections had been worth.

Turning down the volume, Boo-Boo interrupted my train of thought. "Why you fucking with that, nigga?" I snapped.

Pointing towards the foreign car dealership up ahead, he ignored my comment, exclaiming, "Check that pretty shit there out, Chez."

Seeing the vehicle he spoke of, I whipped into the lot with my eyes glued to it.

Grinning as if he already saw himself up in the vehicle, he excitedly stated, "Niggas wouldn't be ready for us if we rode up in that, Bro."

Smiling inwardly, I couldn't help thinking that he had a point. Like Boo-Boo, I too could imagine rolling through in it. Riding up beside it, I quickly exited the whip to take a closer look at the car.

The price was sixteen thousand, but from what I could see, it was well worth it. The Q45 sported a dark green paint job, with interior the color of peanut butter. A set of gold and chrome BBS rims adorned its feet, while the mirror tint on the windows gave the car a look of prestige. It was easy to imagine myself coming through the hood, beating some ole fly shit out of the system I'd immediately install once I purchased it.

"Yo, what you think, Chez? This shit's fly, right?"

My eyes were still glued to the whip as I shook my head. "Yeah, I'm feeling this, man."

"Well, if you're feeling it, buy it then. You know you got the dough," he said, edging me on.

"Excuse me gentlemen, can I help you with anything?" the salesman questioned, appearing from out of nowhere.

Still staring at the car, I said, "We're just checking this joint out, player."

Unlocking the door, he opened it so that we could see inside. Tossing me the keys, he stated, "This is one of the best vehicles I have on the lot. Get in and start it up, so you can see how good you look inside."

Eyeing him suspiciously, it was clear to me that the salesman had game. I could respect good game though, so I sank down into the soft leather interior as I placed the key in the ignition. The digital dash lit up in a futuristic fashion when I turned the key, bringing the luxury car to life. No longer needing guidance to make my decision, I reached in my pocket and extracted a knot. Handing the salesman five grand, I said, "I can be back with the other eleven in an hour. Now the question is, can you make the paper trail on the transaction disappear?"

Chuckling slightly, his face slowly turned serious. "Can I make the paperwork disappear? How about I introduce myself?" Removing his business card, he handed it over.

Grabbing the card, I read the name and smiled. "Well, it looks like we have a deal then, Harry Houdini"

"Mmm, Peanut. You feel so good, baby. Shit!"

"Yeah, bitch! Work your motherfucking ass back!" Groaning with each stroke, Peanut loudly hissed, "Whose ass is this, girl?"

Unable to ignore the ruckus taking place in the next cell due to the thin walls that separated the two barred cubicles, Qwen laid upon the bunk with a look of disgust plastered upon his face. Glaring at the calendar on the wall, he couldn't believe that four years and eleven months of this shit was truly behind him. The piercing moans that rapidly drifted through the walls made him wish that his last 24 hours in this hell hole could have been up 24 hours ago.

"I'm cumming, bitch! Yeah. Daddy's cumming!" Peanut proudly exclaimed at the moment of release.

Shaking his head, Qwen still heard the words he'd been hearing for years with disbelieving ears.

Standing to walk towards the bars, he mumbled, "Faggot motherfuckers!"

No sooner than the words were out of his mouth, he came face to face with someone he knew wouldn't be too happy with what was taking place next door; Peanut's punk's, real man had arrived.

Locking eyes with the young, angry monster, Qwen saw by the red slits in Diesel's face that someone was about to get murdered. Figuring that he wouldn't want to miss the show, Qwen nodded at Diesel and the two thugs that paraded behind him before dropping back down on the cot.

Listening intently from his front row seat, Qwen heard Diesel kick Peanut's bars with the force of a battering ram, blurting, "Send my bitch out of there, nigga, or I'm coming up in there."

Qwen heard feet scurrying on the other side of the thin, sheet-metal wall. Giggling, he couldn't contain the humor of the situation any longer. There was no getting around the fact that they were sick. What part of the game was it that they were actually taught to believe another man was their bitch? Hearing Peanut's reply, Qwen listened closely.

"Coming up in where? I know the fuck you ain't talking about coming up in my shit, nigga."

Snatching the curtain from the bars, Peanut stepped out in the corridor. Ice grilling Diesel and his crew, Peanut growled, "The bitch ain't going nowhere, and you must plan on killing me if you think you're going in there to get her!"

Listening intently to Peanut's defiant words, a sinister grin slowly crept over Diesel's features. Laughing harshly, he flicked his arm, making a long dagger slide quickly from its hiding spot inside his shirt sleeve into his open palm. Slowly approaching Peanut's rapidly evading form, Diesel spoke in a cold, hard tone. "You must be psychic, nigga. I do plan on killing you, then I'm gonna take my time and murder the bitch afterwards."

Rising from the cot, Qwen was just in time to see Peanut dash back inside the cell with Diesel and his men on his heels. No longer able to see what was happening, the sounds of stuff crashing to the floor, followed by bloodcurdling screams alerted him to the massacre that was taking place.

Laying back on the cot, Qwen lit a black and mild and turned the volume up on his radio. Drowning out the noise as much as possible, it wasn't long before the screams subsided. Glancing towards his door, he cut his eyes at the three men who slowly passed. Covered in blood, they halted their steps.

Locking eyes, Diesel asked, "You good, Qwen?"

"I only have 24 hours left in this joint, so you tell me," Qwen replied, blowing out a cloud of smoke.

Momentarily sharing a tense silence, Diesel turned to walk away, but not before tossing over his shoulder, "Keep your head up, homie, and don't change."

Watching them walk away, it dawned on Qwen that Peanut may have been psychic after all. Grinning at the thought, he said, "Fuck Peanut and this raggedy ass penitentiary!"

In 24 hours, he would be starting his life again, and this time he planned to live it to the fullest. Closing his eyes, Qwen didn't know what awaited him when he returned. Nevertheless, he was prepared for whatever.

I had nine ounces, thirteen grand in the safe, and a new sparkling whip parked on the block.

After all I'd accomplished in the last few months, I had a reason to be feeling good. For the first time in my life, things were finally looking up. It was early, so I planned to camp out on the block until I recouped the sixteen grand I'd spent on my whip yesterday. I had my work cut out for me, but I'd decided to politic with the fellows while I handled business.

Tossing some dough on the concrete, I watched Sam shoot for the point that would hopefully assist in refilling my pockets. With Satin, Boo-Boo, Dresser and another twelve or so homies betting heavily themselves, the game was loud and rowdy the way I liked it. Noticing the sudden silence that permeated the air around me, I followed the nervous glares around me to the source. The figure who stood behind me quickly alerted me to exactly what was going on. Qwen was home, and I was sure that like myself, everyone was wondering what type of time he had returned on.

Locking eyes with everyone he passed, Qwen returned each glare with one of his own. Cockily parading through the crowd, it was clear that the years hadn't diminished one iota of his heart, by his gait alone. Reaching the shooter, he tossed a hundred dollar bill on the concrete near Sam. "I'm betting the dice lose."

Seeing the skeptical stares, I grinned inwardly, thinking that his arrival could turn out to be interesting. Unfolding a fat knot, I matched his hundred and tossed it in the center of the group. "I'll take that bet, homie."

Glimpsing the slight manner he eyed me, I solemnly folded my arms across my chest and said, "Let's get this money, Sam."

As nonchalant as I seemed, I was fully aware of the fact that

Qwen was a killer. I'd seen him in action, and like myself, he could blank and put down a vicious murder game when the urge arrived. This was what made me observe him closely, as he found Sam's chrome .45 more interesting than the point he was shooting for. Watching him like a hawk, I awaited his next move.

"Pointed," Sam boasted, reaching around him to snatch up his considerable winnings.

Doing the same, I heard Qwen demand, more than ask, to see Sam's pistol. Glancing upwards, I awaited Sam's reply. Qwen was a nut, but Sam was a fool as well.

Gripping the butt of his pistol firmly, Sam sneered, "No one handles this joint but me." Cutting his eyes as if to say, 'This nigga must be stupid', he asked, "Are there any more faders or is the game over?"

Giving Sam an evil, unblinking stare, Qwen surveyed the crowd as if he were attempting to determine whether he could possibly get away with taking the pistol by force. Deciding against it, he said, "I'll pay whatever it takes if anyone comes across two 45's like his." Turning around, he stalked back through the crowd without a second glance.

Removing my hand from beneath my shirt, where it had been nestled on the trigger of my pistol grip .357, I was glad he hadn't jumped out there foolishly. Even if he had been on some snake shit 5 years ago, I would have hated to put him to sleep when he was fresh out of the penitentiary. Dude deserved another chance, in my book.

Grinning, Qwen didn't even have to turn around to know that too many eyes followed his exit. As planned, he had made his entrance, and that quick, Qwen had easily surmised who ran the show in the hood. It was clear that Lil Sanchez had grown up. Noticing him as soon as he made his entrance, Qwen could see the look in his eyes that spoke of a young warrior. The gun that he slid his hand up under his shirt to grasp, with a smooth, fluid motion hadn't been missed by Qwen either. Realizing that one way or another they would be destined to clash, he decided that he would play the shadows for a while and keep an eye on Chez. As far as Qwen was concerned, the rest of the niggas weren't a threat, but that didn't hold true for Chez. Making a beeline for the phone, he began to dial the number of the little cutie he'd met earlier at the store. Hearing the phone ring, it dawned on him that the nigga, Chez, would either turn out to be a help or hindrance to his future growth in the game.

After pulling my beeper out for the fourth time in as many minutes, I figured I may as well see what Missy's reason for blowing my pager up was. I had planned to camp out on the block for the day, but I'd been avoiding her since I hit it months ago, so I figured a shot of her special head wouldn't be a bad thing.

Making a few sales on my way across the street, I waved Boo-Boo over. "Yo, I need you to take a ride with me, cuz."

"I'm wit' that, playboy."

Hopping in the whip, I watched Boo-Boo throw his favorite tape in the set, lean his seat back and spark an el as if he owned the vehicle. Amused, I had to laugh. When it came to him, either you liked it or you loved it. Boo-Boo had an uncaring way of doing things and that's just the way it was.

Reaching Tracy's house in record time, the loud music must have notified them of our arrival. Before I'd even come to a complete stop, Missy was strutting out the house, looking cute as hell. Opening the door, I sat marveling at the magnitude of just how sexy she was.

Leaning inside the open door, Missy placed a juicy, tongue filled kiss on my mouth, before saying, "I love your new car, boo. This shit is fly!" Scanning the car appreciatively, she playfully hit me. "Why haven't you been calling or coming to see me, nigga?"

Standing, I began to follow her up the walkway. Although I'd cut her back, after hearing that she had been creeping with a nigga I disliked, I chose not to reveal my real reason.

I grasped a handful of her soft ass. "I've been busy as hell, ma. I'm on a mission these days."

Little did she know, I wouldn't be coming around a whole lot more before it was over. In fact, she would be history, real soon.

Entering the house, I immediately made myself comfortable. Dropping down on the couch, Missy made herself just as comfortable as she sat in my lap.

Removing stacks of money from my coat pockets, I tossed a stack to Boo-Boo. "Yo, count that for me, Bro."

Before he could reply, I caught his sudden look of annoyance that was directed behind me. Turning towards whatever his attention had been riveted to, I came face to face with an unexpected guest. Frowning, I couldn't help wondering what the hell he was doing there. Involuntarily sliding my hand beneath my coat to rest upon my burner, I felt Missy's eyes bore into me in a questioning manner at the same time I heard Tracy's words.

"Hey, boy. I didn't know you were here," she said, smiling excitedly. Rubbing Qwen's shoulder affectionately, she chimed in, "I'm glad you are though, because I want you and Boo-Boo to meet my friend, Qwen. He just..."

Cutting her short, I coolly responded, "We've already met." Catching the baffled look that Tracy shared with Missy, I held Qwen's stare as he drained his drink and turned to Tracy.

Grabbing his jacket, Qwen said, "Let's go, Tracy."

Glancing at me with questioning eyes, Tracy followed him to the door as I shrugged my shoulders and smiled.

Reaching the door, Tracy chewed on her bottom lip in exasperation. "Look, Chez. I'm gonna drop him off and come right back. Don't leave, I need to talk to you, okay?"

Nonchalantly replying, "We can do that," I returned my attention back to Missy, who was squirming mischievously in my lap with a lust-filled look on her face.

I had shit to handle, and sitting around waiting on Tracy wasn't on my agenda. However, since Missy would soon be history, I figured I'd better enjoy her while she existed.

"Come on to the back. I need to holler at you."

Ready and willing, she grabbed my hand. "Let's go then."

Following her lead, my eyes caressed her wide swirling hips as I winked at Boo-Boo, saying, "I'll be ready in an hour."

After laying down a vicious freak game, I was back on the block slinging product like a madman. Every one of my pockets was filled with money, and it was crazy to me how in such a short period of time, I had the block on smash. All I could concentrate on at this point, was getting my money up. The way money was flowing through the strip, I had no doubt that getting it was exactly what I was going to do. Turning around at the sound of thunderous music approaching, I came face to face with a group of dudes I wasn't prepared to see. Mann, Dax and Ice were my sworn enemies, and the mean mugs they gave as they pulled up were definitely directed at me. Sliding my hand beneath my shirt to the safety of my baby, I returned their mean glares without a care of what their intentions may have been.

Pulling to a stop directly beside me, Mann transferred the toothpick he was sucking from one side of his mouth to the other. Glaring treacherously, he spoke in a slightly threatening tone. "I see you're rolling solo, tonight. What's up, nigga?" Leaning out the window, he scanned the block suspiciously.

Throwing the disrespectful comment my way, he left no doubt in my mind that he was trying to play me. By the venomous looks Dax and Ice tossed my way, I also had no doubt that the odds were far from being in my favor. Placing my finger inside the trigger guard, I got a firmer hold on my burner, before hissing, "I do my best work alone, nigga. What's up with you?"

Looking at his boys, Mann's eyes then traveled down to the hand I had stuck beneath my shirt. Twisting his face up in anger, he replied, "Nigga, you know how I roll. It's whatever with me."

I already knew they wanted beef, or they wouldn't have even rode through. Ducking it was out of the question, so I pulled back the hammer on my pistol and prepared for gunplay. Locked in a silent staring battle with the three of them, the thought dawned on me that whether I was alone or not, this block was mine. And if it had to come to it, I'd rep it with my life.

Snapping, I said, "Fuck you, nigga! What you want it to be?"

Whipping the Magnum out, I saw the glint of steel being raised in the backseat at the same moment I heard a familiar voice loudly asking, "What's the deal, Bro? If there's a problem, let's get that shit over with."

Seeing Boo-Boo coming out the cut with a pistol dangling in his hand, Mann said, "Nah. Chill fellows," to Dax and Ice, who were ready to set it off.

Staring them down, I spoke calmly as Boo-Boo walked up beside me. "These bitches were just about to leave, cuz. There's no problem, man."

Leaning back inside the car, Mann grinned slyly. "I'll be seeing you, nigga." Neither Dax nor Ice uttered a word, which wasn't unusual because they had a reputation for letting their pistols speak for them. "Be careful, ya hear?" Laughing, Mann turned the system back up and pulled off.

Putting his gun away, Boo-Boo watched the pearl white Cadillac turn the corner. "I hate those bitch ass niggas!" he informed, spitting in the street.

I felt where he was coming from. I hated them as well. But stuff was going too well right now to be having a problem with Mann and his goons. I now had money on my mind, and I planned to keep it that way. This situation brought a lesson to mind that I'd once received from an old hustler, years ago. He had said that only a broke nigga had time for beef, while a paid one couldn't afford to take the loss. Those words suddenly made sense to me, and I damn sure wasn't in the position to be taking any losses.

No longer able to see the caddy, I put my pistol away. "Yo, Boo-Boo, don't trip off those clowns, kid. Let's get our money right and when the time comes to deal with them, we will, alright?"

"Um hmm. We'll definitely handle it," he anxiously retorted. "Only thing is, I can't wait until the time arrives, Chez. I owe them some slugs, and I'm more than ready to pay the debt."

In the shadows, Qwen stood with a Glock in each hand. His mission had been to see how Chez was stacking his cheddar, in case it came down to having to relieve him of it. Only now, there had suddenly been a change of plans at the sight of one of his past enemies. Watching Mann and the dilemma Chez faced through angry little slits, he had impatiently waited to see how the homie would handle himself. Flicking the safeties on the Glocks, he listened closely to hear Chez's rebuttal, because if he had to handle the problem for him, he would have gladly left the street leaking.

From his hidden position in the shadows, Qwen heard everything that had taken place. Intrigued, he had to give Chez his due respect. Placing his weapons back in his waist, it was now clear that he was correct in his assumption of Chez. By going up against Mann, who Qwen hated, but knew was a killer, Chez had shown himself to have big heart. BooBoo had also caught his eye, making the both of them stand out from the rest of the dudes who Qwen felt were running around the 3rd Ward frontin'.

Quietly backing away from the pair who stood in conversation, oblivious to his close proximity to them, Qwen came to the conclusion that he was in need of a crew like the two of them. Although they didn't realize it at the moment, he decided that they needed him on their team as well. Thinking fast, the only question Qwen had was, how could they link up?

Hanging up the phone, I was astounded to say the least. Leaving the room where Monya and my daughter slept, I made my way to the living room. After the surprise call from Satin, I needed to think. Taking a seat, the conversation we'd just had replayed itself in my mind. Why he was suddenly ready to take the trip to New York now, I would more than likely never know. Yet, what I did know that I was ready, regardless of what his reasons were. As it stood, I had right at eighteen thousand to cop with. The sixteen gees I'd spent on the car would have helped out greatly, but even with the lesser amount, I would only be a few ounces shy of a key when we returned.

Closing my eyes, it was only natural that I reflected back to where I was just a few months ago, in comparison to where I stood at the present and planned to be in the future. Smiling excitedly, it was clear that my come up was official, and this was no more than the beginning. Feeling that so much more awaited, I couldn't help wondering what else fate had planned for me on my rise.

Chapter 6

Reaching in the ashtray, I pulled out a partially smoked blunt and lit it. Savoring the smooth taste, I blew out a cloud of smoke and turned the music up. I was halfway to New York, and even though I was high as hell, driving throughout the night had me tired. With no one to talk to, I was finding it hard to stay awake due to the boredom I was experiencing. It had been a long time since I'd taken this trip up 95, and after glancing out the corner of my eye at Satin's sleeping form, it became clear that tired or not, I was the designated driver.

Looking at the clock, I figured that if everything went according to my earlier calculations, we would arrive in the city around daybreak. Shaking my head to clear my focus, I smiled at the realization that in a few hours, I would be one step closer to reaching my goals. Seeing the Maryland House rest stop sign ahead, I changed lanes. After refilling the tanks and stretching my legs, I looked forward to our next stop. New York City awaited us.

Playfully pushing Satin's head against the passenger window, I spat, "Get up nigga, we're here."

Squinting his sleep filled eyes, he rubbed them, then asked, "Where we at?"

Frowning at his foolish question, the thought came to mind that not even he was country enough to not recognize where the hell we were. "Where the hell you think we're at fool? We're in New York City, man."

"Whatever nigga!" Sitting up to get a better view of his surroundings, Satin asked, "What part of the City are we in?"

"You're now in the heart of Washington Heights," I stated proudly. "This is where the majority of the coke on the East coast originates from, my man. Welcome to Broadway, nigga.'"

Peering lustfully at the array of Puerto Rican dime pieces that littered the sidewalks as we passed, his reply was, "Damn!"

Unsure of whether his reply was to my statement or the sweet view, I smiled. Loving myself some Puerto Rican women as well, I could appreciate his undivided attention being on them at the moment.

"Are we there yet, baby?" the tired voice behind us questioned in a low tone.

Glancing in the backseat, it hit me once again that we were playing a dirty game. The sight of the old lady, sitting submissively behind me was sad. Shaking my head, I was too disgusted at the realization that my partner using his own Grandmother as our mule.

Uninterested in anything she had to say, Satin barked, "Yeah, we're here, Damn!" Cutting short any other questions she may have had, he turned to me. "Who you planning to cop from, Chez?"

This was the good part. I had never taken the time to explain that I had no connect in the city. Grinning inwardly, I figured that at this point it really didn't matter. Staring straight ahead, I shrugged my shoulders. "Your guess is as good as mine, cuz. We'll find somebody."

From the corner of my eye, I could see his face twist into an angry mask. "What?" he yelled angrily. "Hell nah! Man, I know you didn't bring me all the way up here without any idea of who we're gonna score from."

Staring at him as if he had lost his damn mind, I quickly came to the conclusion that whether he was my boy or not, I would pull the car over and do something big with him if he got out of hand.

Whispering in an attempt to mask my own rising anger, I said, "You better tighten up and watch your tone of voice, nigga. We're here. We're gonna get what we came for, and that's that." Receiving no response, I added, "Where we're headed, there's more than enough coke for sale. Believe me man, the last thing we have to worry about is getting served."

Still pissed off, Satin said, "Yeah, alright. I don't like it, but I've come this far, and I damn sure don't plan on going home empty handed. We'll do it your way." Turning up the volume on the radio, he swiveled towards the passenger window and focused his attention back on the passing scenery.

Figuring that he was in his feelings, I reached over and turned the radio up a few more decibels. Fuck his feelings! Bopping my head to Redman's joint, it dawned on me that like the words that loudly blared from the speakers; I too felt that it was time for some action.

After driving all night, then running around with over forty-five thousand in search of a legitimate connect all day; I was ready to drop. Choosing to wait in the car, Satin had left me no other option than to put all the work in alone. So much for bringing him along, when he ended up serving no purpose whatsoever.

I ended up finding a Dominican connect, who from the looks of it had much more product than I could ever expect to purchase. Bargaining like a Wall Street stockbroker, I was able to return to the car within an hour, carrying two keys of diamond encrusted fishscale. Tossing them in Satins lap, I witnessed his nervous look of indecision turn to immediate excitement. Slightly frowning in his unseeing direction, I made a silent oath that this would be the last trip his selfish, soft ass would ever be making with me. I was in possession of my first key and there was no doubt in my mind that with it, the game had changed.

Dropping Satin's grandmother at the Port Authority bus terminal, we watched from a safe distance as she boarded the bus, headed to Richmond, Va.

With that part of the plan safely executed, it was time to hit the highway. Needing to be in place when the bus arrived in Richmond, I was prepared to get there.

Seething inside, I couldn't stop glancing in Satin's direction. Even though he was supposed to be driving back, he sat slumped in the passenger seat with his head resting against the window, snoring lightly. Once again, instead of handling his responsibilities, he had spent the day smoking coke cigarettes. Now, here I was again, pulling his weight along with my own. Sighing, it became clear to me that when we returned home, some major changes would have to be made.

Boo-Boo had-already brought it to my attention that Satin was back smoking, but at that point, it hadn't made any real difference to me. Things were now different because it was cutting into my business. Therefore, seeing the collision course he was headed towards, I planned to make the necessary changes that would insure I didn't go down along with him. If I was gonna succeed, Satin had to go.

The trip came off like clockwork; I'd made it home safely, whipped up my product, made love to my woman, and showered. With a key and a half in the stash and no money, the 48 hours without sleep no longer mattered. It was time to refill the safe. Until that was done, sleep would have to wait.

Knowing that there was a serious shortage of coke in the city, I realized that having it my way with mine was a must. With that thought in mind, I cruised through the strip on a mission to open shop. I'd bagged up five thousand nickel bags, that would bring in an immediate $25,000 dollars once the dealers found out the work was available. And it had only taken thirteen ounces to recoup my original investment, plus some.

On top of the world, I couldn't believe how sweet the new year had been. I had a newborn baby girl, a luxury whip and an attitude to match. The key and five ounces I had left in the cut was a plus. Turning onto Mistletoe Street, I decided that before I went back to New York, I was gonna buy Monya a new car and move my little family into a more luxurious place.

Pulling to the curve, I spotted two cuties lounging on the porch. Rhonda and Fat Baby were sisters, and the way they were swaying to the sounds blaring from my vehicle, I knew that my company would be more than welcome. Exiting the infinity with the bag filled with coke dangling in my hand, I strolled towards them.

"What's up with the two finest ladies in the hood?" I questioned in my customary flirtatious manner, taking a seat between them.

Scooting further apart, they each responded, "Hey Chez."

Making room for me to sit comfortably, Rhonda replied, "We're just sitting out here, tripping off the way these crackheads are walking around searching for a hit like zombies."

Fat Baby then chinned. "Ain't nobody got shit around here either, Chez." Staring down at the bag that sat between us, she cracked, "From the looks of it, that's no longer the case though."

"That's correct," I stated, grinning. "We're about to get real busy, so who wants to drink with the kid? Nah. My bad, ya'll don't drink. Do you?" I teased.

"Hell yeah!" They replied in unison.

Pointing towards the car, I said "I'm not gonna buy it and serve your asses too. One of you better go get that shit."

Rising from the steps, to go retrieve the drinks, Fat Baby playfully popped me. "Shut up, boy, I'll get it," she informed, gliding sexily down the steps.

From the dark spot Qwen stood in, he had a clear view of Chez. Seeing him arrive on the block, Qwen made his way through the back alley to crouch out of sight between the row houses. No longer interested in robbing him, Qwen didn't really know what to do next. He had been home a week already, and no one had even attempted to hit him off, or throw him anything. Besides Tracy, he didn't even have any friends. At this point, it was about getting money and making moves as far as he was concerned. In his eyes Chez was ballin', and more than anything, Qwen wanted in. Ready to initiate a meeting between them, Qwen stepped from the shadows and awaited his chance.

Thinking that I would love to get a hold of Fat Baby, I followed her forward progress to retrieve the alcohol with my eyes glued to her deliciously rounded bottom. Enchanted by the sway of her hips, I squirmed on the steps, calling out, "Bring the cups from the backseat too, baby."

Not wanting my motives to seem too obvious, I forced my attention back to Rhonda who was sitting entirely too quietly beside me. Immediately noticing her intense glare in the other direction, I nosily followed her stare to the opposite side of the street.

Meeting my gaze, Qwen acknowledged me with a slight nod of the head as he nonchalantly smoked a cigarette. I returned the greeting, while wondering to myself what the hell he was doing in the shadows this time of night. Strapped and fearless, I just figured that maybe he was on the grind; other than that, I let his arrival slip from my mind.

In no time flat, I was in the swing of the late night rush. The fiends and hustlers from my strip had me surrounded. Word had traveled fast, and the product was moving at a lightning pace. Dudes were coping big.

Between the straight cups of Henny, getting money, and talking trash, the time had flown by. Although my workers had taken the majority of the product I'd brought out, for the hell of it, I had sold a few thousand dollars' worth, hand to hand. Enjoying the flow and feeling good, I still kept a close eye on Qwen, who I was positive hadn't let me out of his sight either. It was funny to me, because whether he was aware or not, I had plans for him, and it was time to embark upon them. Figuring that my bag only held about 300 or so nickel sacks, I looked across the street and held the bottle of Hennessy up, waving for him to come over. Seeing his slight look of hesitation, I inwardly grinned when he began to move towards me.

Watching his steady approach, I could see the indecision in his eyes. Deciding to break the ice, I said, "Welcome home, man." Pushing the bottle in his direction, I added, "Take this shit, player; I can't drink it all by my damn self."

Taking the bottle from my outstretched hand, he took a swig, frowning at the obvious burn the liquor produced as it traveled down his throat. Hitting it again, he handed it back. Looking around him, he said, "Thanks, man, it's been a long time since I've stood out here and drank some good liquor."

Hitting the bottle again myself, I chuckled, "It's nothing, my man." Taking note of the cheap gear he was wearing, I had to ask. "You out here getting your grind on, homie?"

Breaking eye contact, he looked off into the distance, "Nah man, I haven't been able to get on yet. You already know how it is, I'm sure."

Shaking my head yeah, I really couldn't understand his situation, for real. His brother ran around the city acting like a baller and here he was out here broke. Seeing my opening, I asked, "What is it that you've been trying to get?"

Thinking on it, Qwen responded, "I've only been trying to get a half ounce, player. A nigga needs some gear," he added, throwing his arms out as if to say look at me.

Eyeballing him, it was easy to see that he was down on his luck. I too had been there, and the only difference was, I wasn't gonna allow him to stay down. I'd already decided to bring him up. He was a soldier, and I needed him on my team.

Pushing the bottle back in his hand, I gave him a stern look. "Yo, I'll tell you what I'm gonna do. You help me finish this bottle off, and I got you."

Allowing a glimmer of a smile to appear, he lifted the bottle to his lips. "I'm not doing anything else." Taking a short sip, his eyes traveled admiringly over my whip. "I like that joint, man."

Reaching for the rapidly vibrating pager on my hip, I casually said, "Thanks, man." Coming to the conclusion that a cell phone was very necessary, I tossed him my keys. "Let's roll, player. I gotta go call this worrisome ass female."

Catching the keys, Qwen hesitantly looked at them, before staring at the car then back at me.

Smirking at the look on his face, I teasingly asked, "You can drive, right?"

"Umm hmm, I can drive, but..."

Cutting him off, I said, "But nothing. Let's ride, playboy." Turning to Rhonda and Fat baby, I winked my eye. "You two hold it down out here and I'll holler back, okay?" Jumping in the passenger seat, I turned the music up, oblivious to any reply they may have uttered.

We rode around for over an hour, conversing about the past, present and future. My mind was completely made up where he was concerned; it was a go. I'd gladly do something for a real dude straight out the pen, before I'd give something to one of the sorry ones who constantly stood around with their hands out. Qwen was hungry, and I could see it in his eyes. I would make sure that he ate well, and I had no doubt that his loyalty would follow.

Arriving back on the block, I jumped in the drivers' seat and tossed him the bag. "Get you some money, man. You don't owe me nothing." Placing the car in drive, I informed him, "I'll see you tomorrow."

Pulling off before he could reply, I watched the excited look he shot my way in the mirror as he looked in the bag.

Raising the volume on the system, I felt good as I cruised through the deserted streets. Reaching in the ashtray, I sparked a partially lit blunt and inhaled. Once again, I found myself to be the designated driver. Only this time, it was cool. I was on my way home to the two women I loved most. My pockets were overflowing with gee stacks, and I had a new soldier on the team. Smiling, it was clear that with me behind the wheel, a future come up was not just realistic, but inevitable.

Chapter 7

Summer '92

I was finally able to drag myself away from Mia, after a long evening of being held hostage by her professional freak techniques. Sighing at the thought alone, I had to admit that she had the ability to relieve me of any unneeded stress, while putting a little extra pep in my step.

Having called Qwen before I left Mia, I had my eyes peeled for him as I headed towards our rendezvous spot on Broad Street. Like myself, his good looks made him an instant hit with the females. Around 5'10", Qwen had a pecan complexion, curly, short hair and a chiseled, muscular physique. After taking him along on one of my visits to see Mia, he was immediately snatched up by her best friend Tishaun. Now that she had him, I was sure that she would be hanging on to him for dear life when I arrived at our rendezvous spot.

Checking my watch, I found that I was on point. Grinning at the attention drawn to Monya's new Maxima, it hit me that these days I was on point with every aspect of my life. My money was stacking. Niggas in my clique were eating. Our weight was up, and for the first time in my life, I was truly happy.

One of my greatest accomplishments, as far as I was concerned, was snatching Qwen up. Just as I thought; he had turned into my most loyal ally, more like a big brother to be exact. Unlike the Qwen of five years before, he was turning out to be the fastest growing money maker in the city. Not even his past reputation as a certified robber and murderer could hinder his rapid growth. If anything, it seemed to be his prior reputation that assisted in fueling the growth he was experiencing.

With the exception of a few vicious slaps, I'd seen no proof of any adversity or opposition from any of his street soldiers. That being the case, I'd never had to raise a finger to intervene on his behalf since we hooked up.

Approaching the stoplight, I caught sight of him and Tishaun up ahead. Caught by the red light, I couldn't help staring at the two of them. Standing near the car with Tishaun's arms possessively wrapped around his neck as she smilingly leaned into him, it hit me that this was deja-vu. This was the same way he had been five years ago, when I watched his wrath unfold as a little shorty. Drifting into thought, the events were just as clear to me now, as if it were 1987.

5 years before

The evening sun was slowly drifting into the clouds, making way for the cooling summer breeze. With the blazing sun's disappearance, all who had hidden in air conditioned comfort throughout the day slowly began to make their appearance on the block. Like them, I too found this to be the best time of the day to hit the strip.

Making my way up the block, I looked forward to the night's festivities. Like every other night that I had made my entrance, the loud music blaring from an array of fly whips with even flyer honeys dancing beside them, gave notice that with the night breeze, the party had begun.

Stopping to holler at a group of my partners, I found myself drawn to the sight they were locked on. Openly gawking like the rest, I lustfully stared at the stacked, chocolate chick who leaned against one of my older homies. Nothing my young eyes had seen up to this point could begin to compare to her assets. Thinking that Qwen was the coolest dude on earth at that moment, I swallowed a mouthful of saliva and wished I could be like him.

In the time I had taken to blink, it seemed as if the whole block had gone haywire. Out of nowhere, gunshots began ringing out, as dudes ran and females screamed in panic. The Bronco the young assassins traveled in screeched to a halt near Qwen. At the same moment, I witnessed my dream girl crumble in his arms, with the left side of her head missing. In shock, I stood rooted in my spot and watched the masked men jump from the truck and snatch Qwen at gun point.

In seconds, he was inside, and they were speeding away. Just when I knew he would never be seen alive again, the loud roar of a gun could be heard. The blood that splattered against the windshield had to belong to the driver, because the Bronco's altered course into a house couldn't have been intentional. Once the truck crashed, more gunshots could be heard from inside. From my vantage point, I was the first one to see the door open as one of the masked men fell from the vehicle. Injured and staggering, he attempted to make his escape. Figuring that everyone else inside was dead, I stared in awe as Qwen emerged from the wreck, bloody, with a black 9 in each of his hands.

In a rage, Qwen hollered, "Nigga, you want to fuck with me?" as he fired a shot from each weapon into the lower torso of the fleeing assassin. Dropping him on his face, he quickly caught up to the masked man. Kicking him in the head with bone crushing force, Qwen screamed, " You bitches actually thought you could kill me, motherfucker!"

Whimpering incoherently, the masked man just laid there in a manner of defeat.

With a cold chill in his tone, Qwen snapped loud enough for everyone assembled to hear. "Let this serve as a lesson to anyone who thinks I'm not about mine." Staring downwards with a look of pure hatred, he began to simultaneously fire both weapons into the face and chest of his supposed assassin. After both guns were empty, he hawked and spat on the bloody corpse, before turning nonchalantly and strolling up the middle of the block...

"Bump! Bump! Bump!" Snapping out of my thoughts at the sound of honking horns, it was wild to me that even after all the blood, brains, and guts I'd seen since then, that particular day had stuck in my mind. Shaking my head, I had to laugh at the way they stood smiling foolishly at me as I approached. Apparently they had witnessed my lack of attention at the stoplight. I couldn't help it if my mind had drifted back to the first and only time I'd witnessed a unarmed man go up against three armed men and come away unscathed.

Pulling beside them, I lowered the window. "Hey Tishaun." Grinning at her obvious hesitation to release Qwen, I said, "You rolling with me, or are you on lock-down, nigga?"

Raising his brow, Qwen quickly retorted, "I'm rolling with you, bro." Winking his eye over her unseeing head, he lied, "She already knows I'd gladly stay with her if you didn't need me to handle that business for you."

Smiling slyly, I decided to mess with him. "Well, if I'm the reason you have to go, we can always put our business off til —"

Quickly cutting me short, Qwen said, "Give me a kiss, baby. I'll give you a call tomorrow, alright?"

Rolling her eyes in my direction, she pouted, "Umm hmm,

Qwen." Leaning in for a juicy kiss, Tishaun whispered, "You better call me too, boy."

Breaking away, Qwen rushed to get in the car. "You know I will, girl." Closing the door, he mumbled, "Pull off, you dirty motherfucker," without losing his smile or moving his mouth.

Unable to control my laughter, I whipped out of the parking lot before I laughed in Tishaun's face.

Bursting into laughter himself, Qwen said. "That's fucked up, bro. You already know she got a white liver and you pull some shit like that." Becoming serious, he admitted, "She's a monster, Chez. And even though I like chillin' with her, when it's time to go, I'm ready."

Laughing even harder at the serious look that sat on his face, I could only imagine how freaky she really was. Picking, I said, "If you need some help with her, I'll gladly step in."

Removing the cigarette he'd just placed in his mouth, Qwen replied, "You have my blessings, nigga. But I have a feeling that your hands are full enough with Mia."

Shaking my head, I couldn't argue that. What I saw at that moment, on the other side of the street, made me quickly forget about Mia or any other female for that matter. My hands could never be too full to make room for another one like the one I now had in my sights.

Whipping into the far lane, I made a sharp U-turn. My mind had been on Neeta for months, and I was about to lay my gangster down hard this time. I wanted her bad, and tonight she would know it.

Blowing out a cloud of smoke, Qwen calmly asked, "What the hell are you doing, man?" as I pulled up behind the Mercedes and Honda parked curbside.

Pointing to the assembled group of women and dudes who watched the Maxima suspiciously, I said, "I gotta have lil' mama over there, so I'm going to get her." Placing my pistol in my waist, I grinned, "Just watch my back in case I have to act a fool."

Reaching for his own burner, Qwen responded, "You already know that, Chez." Glancing at the assembled group, I could tell by their astounded looks that they had no idea who was inside the crème Maxima, with tinted windows and chrome rims. There was no way that they could have known that I had just purchased it.

Smiling at the thought, I placed a fake scowl on my face and exited the vehicle, followed by Qwen. Catching everyone off guard, I snapped "What the fuck is going on out here?" Mean mugging the dudes who seemed not to know what to make of the situation, I barked, "Bring your ass here, Neeta!"

Looking at me with a mixture of embarrassment and fear etched upon her features, Neeta started walking towards me as her girls giggled behind her.

Instead of laughing at the irony of the situation like I wanted to, I edged it on further by raising my Polo tee-shirt over the handle of the 9 millimeter that sat in the waistband of my Guess shorts. This move was more for the eyes of their male counterparts than anything else. The way I saw it, they needed to know I was strapped in case one of them wanted her bad enough to play hero.

Reaching me, Neeta nervously whispered, "Chez, what do you call yourself doing?"

Face to face with the woman who I'd been thinking about ever since our last meeting, I could only think, Umph, Umph, Umph. She was a true beauty and she knew it. Around 5'2' maybe 5'3', Neeta was the picture of perfection. Brown skinned, with hazel eyes, long hair, a phat ass and some of the widest hips I'd ever seen on a woman of her stature, I refused to believe that she hadn't been created specifically for me.

Placing her hands on what I had already pegged as my hips, she defiantly sucked her teeth. "Do you plan to stand here and stare at me the rest of the night, or are you gonna tell me what you call yourself doing?"

Unconvinced by her slight show of irritation, I gave her a sly smile. "What I'm gonna do is act a fool out here, any minute now, if you don't make me understand why you never called me.

Reaching for my weapon, I raised my voice an octave. "Which one of these niggas you fucking with? Huh?" I glared angrily.

Smiling, she grabbed my hand. "Please don't make a scene out here, Chez, please," she pleaded. "I'll call your crazy ass; I promise, I will."

Admiring the way she was packed into the tight bodysuit, I began to smile as well. "So you're gonna give a nigga a call, huh?" Raising my brow playfully, I stared into her alluring eyes. "When do you plan on making that call, ma?"

Matching my stare, she blushed, "I promise not to let another day pass without using your number, alright?"

Reaching for the gun, I felt her soft hand grasp mine. Cutting her eyes devilishly, she grinned, "you know you're wrong, Chez."

Catching her off guard, I pulled her to me and placed a gentle kiss upon her soft, glossy lips. Breaking the kiss, I slowly began backpedaling towards the Maxima. Holding our eye contact, I said. "go on back to your friends, just make sure I hear from you tomorrow."

Getting back in the car, I pulled off to the sound of Qwen's laughter. Catching his breath, he shook his head and said, "You're a fool, Chez. Who the hell was she, anyway?"

Wiping the smile from my face, I gave him the most serious look I could muster. "My man, after tonight she's my newest creation."

Locked on the slowly departing Maxima, Neeta scrutinized Chez's obvious newfound wealth with a level of admiration. Dreamily, she could clearly see that life was looking up for him. Through her association with numerous ballers, it was easy for Neeta to tell when a nigga was headed in an upward spiral; without a doubt that was what she saw happening with him.

"Hey, girl. You coming back over here with us, or are you scared Chez might come back?" Paulette questioned, followed by the laughter of the assembled group.

Smiling at their humor, she stared off into the distance before turning in the direction of her friends. Slowly strolling toward them, Neeta's mind was doing somersaults. Deciding that the time had come to get at Chez, she realized that just maybe he could assist her in her pursuit of a higher lifestyle adjustment.

Chapter 8

Reaching for another Corona, I sighed at the thought of the task that lay ahead of me. Savoring the ice cold beer, my eyes unconsciously scanned the contents of the table in front of me. After spending over an hour calculating money, we had over 80 grand before us. Staring at the perfectly piled stacks, I couldn't help but grin.

Smirking at the look on my face, Qwen joked, "You make a pretty picture sitting there surrounded by all those Benjamins, nigga."

Laughing at his statement, I picked the blunt up from the ashtray and took a drag. Exhaling a miniature smoke cloud, I asked, "What time are our flight reservations, bro?"

Checking his watch, Qwen said, "We have a boarding call for seven o'clock, so we need to start getting ready. Tara and Michelle checked in too. They said that they're ready to hit the highway whenever you are."

"Okay. Things seem to be in order then."

Rubbing my eyes, I reached for a bag to place the money in as I stood. Glancing at my own watch, I wasn't surprised to find that only an hour and a half remained before our flight took off.

Shaking my head, I commented, "It looks like we'll be late as usual, unless we get the show on the road right now."

Pulling out his phone and flipping it open, Qwen said, "I'll call the girls and let them know we're ready."

Watching him walk in another room, I grinned at the precise way he went about handling business. Grabbing my twin four-fifths, I strapped them on effortlessly while scouring the table in search of my phone.

Finding it, I dialed Monya's phone to check in before leaving town. Listening to the ringing phone, I mentally went through the long checklist of things that needed to be done.

"Hello," a sweet voice spoke in a casual tone.

Instantly grinning at the sound of Monya's voice, I responded, "How's my baby?"

The smile was evident in her tone when she replied, "Oh, hey, boo. I'm on my way to the mall. What you doing?"

Already subtracting the amount I knew she was about to spend, I smiled at the thought that whatever made her happy was fine with me.

"Baby, guess what? Nah. On second thought, I may as well just break the news to you myself. I'm on my way out of town, so I won't be seeing you and my little one until tomorrow."

Whining, Monya huffed, "No, Chez. I don't want you to go, baby."

Smiling at her antics, I chuckled, "I have no choice, ma. I gotta make these trips in order for you to continue buying out the mall like you do."

"Baby, you're wrong," Monya laughed. "But since you put it like that, I understand. You just be careful and hurry home, alright?"

"I'll try my best, baby. Kiss my little one, and I'll see you tomorrow, ma."

"Okay." Pouting in her sexy voice, Monya said, "I love you, Chez."

"Same here, baby. I gotta go." Hanging up the phone, I heard Qwen's footsteps behind me.

"It's a go, man. The women are ready. So whose car are we taking, yours or mine?" Qwen asked.

"As tired as I am, that's easy, partner."

Grabbing the bag of money, I began walking towards the door. "We're riding in that pretty, new Acura Legend of yours." Smiling to myself, I yawned, "Let's go, nigga."

Meeting up with my mules, Tara and Michele, I gave them their directions and placed the money and weapons in the stash box for safe transport. Now I could relax, knowing that my weapons and money would be waiting for me in New Jersey when I arrived. Having them on my team insured the safe transport of my product, as the highway patrol more or less turned a blind eye to beautiful women who traveled up and down I-95.

Heading to Byrd Airport after sending them on their way, I relaxed in the knowledge that everything was on point. Leaning back in the butter soft interior of Qwen's Acura, I was not only proud of my achievements, but impressed with those he had made in a short period of time as well. The life we were living was nothing short of a dream, and there was no doubt in my mind that someone was watching over us.

Arriving at the airport, we parked and hurried through the terminal. As usual, we were late. And as usual, my phone was ringing. Reaching in my pocket, I snatched it out. "Yeah, this is Chez. You're on the clock, so make it fast," I blurted into the receiver.

Giggling, Neeta replied, "You got me on the clock now? Yeah, right. Imagine that. Where you at, boo?"

"Damn right, you're on the clock. And it's ticking fast, so what you want?" I questioned, with a grin plastered on my face. Hearing her slight intake of breath, I knew that a stink reply was on the way.

"What?" she questioned, with bitterness in her tone. "You must have me mixed up with another one of your bitches, Chez." Babbling on, Neeta said, "Ticking my ass, nigga. You had better recognize who I am," she angrily stated in a quivering voice.

Turned on by her feisty temper, I switched gears, allowing my charm to take over. "How is daddy's beautiful baby doing? You know I miss you, don't you?"

Pouting, she responded, "No you don't miss me, Chez." Sighing, Neeta said, "I need to see you tonight, baby. I miss you..."

Cutting her short, I replied, "I'm sorry to have to break the bad news to you, but it's not gonna happen, baby."

"Why?" she whined. "Damn, Chez! You haven't spent any time with me all week."

Waving to me, Qwen frowned, "Come on, man. Our plane is boarding."

"Yeah, yeah. I'm coming," I responded. Covering the receiver, I mumbled "It's Neeta."

"Come on, Bro. You gotta wrap your conversation up, so we can make our flight."

"Look here, baby, I can't make it tonight. I'll explain later because if I don't cut this call short, my plane will be leaving without me."

As if she hadn't heard my words clearly the first time, Neeta launched into an array of questions. "Where you going, Chez? Why aren't you taking me? And when are you coming back?"

Removing the phone from my ear, I said, "Damn!" Figuring that she had no intentions of shutting up, I cut in, "I gotta go, boo, but I'll be sure to bring you something back."

Hanging up before she had even finished speaking, I shook my head in Qwen's direction.

"You wanted her, and now you have her," he laughed. Playfully slapping my shoulder, he smirked, "Between her and Monya, you definitely have your hands full, bro."

Smiling at his comment, I had to admit, he had a point. Now I just hoped that they never bumped heads. I wanted them both, and that was one problem that I wasn't prepared to deal with.

Holding the dead phone, Neeta snapped, "Oh, no he didn't just hang up on me." Sucking her teeth, she was in the process of dialing him back when she pushed the end button in mid dial. Tossing her long hair over her shoulders, an even better idea came to mind. Rummaging through her memory bank, Neeta popped her fingers at the sudden recollection of the number she sought. Quickly punching them in, she awaited the answer that she knew would gladly bring a level of excitement and financial gain her way.

"What!" the deep voice boomed on the other end.

Responding in her sexiest tone, Neeta purred, "Hey there, handsome. Oh, and there's no such thing as what when it comes to me. It's more like whatever you want, whenever you need it."

Laughing, he said, "What up, Neeta? How much is this call gonna cost me? And how hard do you plan to get down for my dough?"

"Well, let's just say I'm prepared to get as down and dirty as I have to. As for the cost, you already know I'm high maintenance, so don't even come unless you can give me mine according to how much the bankroll weighs, baller. I'm far from the few hundred dollar escapade, baby." Grinning at her confident words, she knew that the trick on the other end wanted her regardless of what the cost would be.

"Oh, is that so?" he smugly questioned. "Here's the deal then, shawty. I got the dough your high maintenance ass needs. But being as though I haven't heard from you in such a long time, I expect you to pull out all the stops for my loot. Hear me good, Neeta. Tonight there's no holds barred, alright?"

Quickly tossing back a reply, Neeta coolly stated, "Not only is it alright, it's all good, nigga. I expect you to be here in no more than an hour," she informed, ending their call. Dropping the phone on the couch, Neeta began to laugh in a bitter tone.

In deep thought, she wondered if Chez really believed she was one of those young, foolish, in love with the hype type bitches. If so, she had a serious wakeup call in store for him when the time came. As far as Neeta was concerned, love was for lames and suckers. Her definition of love was having bank; plenty of it to be exact. Therefore, regardless of who she had to fuck or cross, Neeta would continue to live for the only thing she really loved; money.

Meeting the ladies in Jersey, we retrieved the money and weapons from the stash spot. Depositing them in the Airport Marriott, we embarked upon our business that waited in New York. Uneasy about handling my business at night, I changed my mode of operation this time in order to meet my connect's boss. Never one to fear the unknown, I still wasn't feeling too good about changing what had worked just fine for me up to this point. The only thing that boosted my confidence was the two forty-fives I carried, and the knowledge that my partner was strapped with two loaded Glocks.

Reaching the meeting spot, we parked directly in front of the Broadway restaurant. Although Qwen hadn't spoken of any doubts he may have been having, I noticed how he double parked, so that no other vehicles would be able to block ours. Seeing this, I immediately knew that he had taken precautions in case we were forced to make a hasty getaway.

Quietly making a last minute check of my weapons, I placed them back in their shoulder straps. Glancing at Qwen, I said, "Let's make it happen, bro."

With no more words needed, we exited the vehicle and strolled towards the restaurant.

No sooner than we entered, the loud salsa music immediately assaulted my eardrums. There was a sparse crowd inside, but even with such a small gathering, they were partying at a feverish pace. Slowly strolling further into the interior of the restaurant, our eyes were treated to an array of Latin asses and breasts, rapidly jiggling in every perceivable direction.

Grinning slyly, I could tell by the lustful gaze in Qwen's eyes that he too was receiving immense enjoyment from the gorgeous women in view. Feeling a hand grasp my shoulder, I quickly turned in the direction of the culprit, thinking that I'd allowed myself to lose focus. Coming face to face with my connect, Carlos, I un-balled my fist and allowed the evil look on my face to soften.

"I'm glad you made it safely," he said, leaning closer so I could hear him above the blaring music. Patting my back, he instructed, "Follow me."

Walking in step with Carlos, I noticed an older gentleman sitting at a back table alone. What drew my attention to him was his regal appearance and the diamond encrusted crucifix that shot sparks as it hung low upon his chest. At first glance I was aware of the power he held, and it was suddenly clear to me that this was the man I was summoned to meet.

Arriving at the table, I never relinquished the eye contact we had held from the moment I'd first noticed him sitting alone.

"Bocca, this is who I've been talking about," Carlos nervously stated, before turning to me. "Chez, I'd like you to meet my boss, Bocca Chula."

Before I could respond, he stood and reached for my hand. Grasping it in a tight, vise-like grip, he spoke in a voice that was clear and sincere. "It's my pleasure to make your acquaintance, Chez." Pulling out a chair beside the one he had been sitting in, Bocca said, "Let's have a seat and discuss affairs."

I was taken aback by his excellent English. It was apparent by his fluent way of speaking that I was no longer in the presence of the prodigal-drug dealer. Carlos was cool, but Bocca's demeanor alone, was proof enough for me to conclude that this meeting was the beginning of something more.

Taking the seat he offered, I pointed to Qwen. "This here is my brother, Qwen. I trust him with my life, so I hope that you have no problem with him sitting in on our discussion."

"No problem at all, my friend. If he's with you, he's with me," Bocca stated fluently. "Hold on a moment." Stopping a passing waitress who in my opinion should have been a model, he commanded, "Bring us two bottles of your best Champagne."

Allowing her to get out of earshot, he picked up where he'd left off. "I asked Carlos to call this meeting because Virginia is a market I want to reach, and he speaks very highly of you. From the sounds of it, you seem to be doing well for yourself. However, I feel that it would benefit us both a lot more if we were to work out a way to get money together." Lighting a thin cigar, he leaned back and awaited my reply.

Ecstatic at the possibility of a union with Bocca, I played it cool and replied in as nonchalant a manner as I could, "I hear what you're saying, but what amount of product are we talking about? Also, what kind of prices do you have in mind that could possibly be beneficial to me? I'm not trying to undermine you in any way, Bocca, but I'm in a major position as it is without a partner." Watching him closely, I eagerly awaited his response.

"I understand the position you're in, Chez." Halting our conversation while the waitress placed the bottles on the table, he nodded his head in thanks, then continued. "Realizing your position is what lets me know that I can make you even more powerful than you could have ever imagined." Pouring himself a drink, he allowed his words to sink in before speaking. "What have you come to purchase on this trip, my friend?"

"I'm prepared to buy four keys at the usual twenty thousand dollar ticket," I stated, allowing my eyes to scan the interior of the restaurant. I couldn't quite put my finger on it, but something had my internal alarms sounding.

"I see," Bocca said, calculating in his head. Taking a sip of champagne, he grinned, "Let's say I front you ten kilos for starters, at sixteen five a piece. The eighty grand you were prepared to spend will be used as a retainer against the amount of my front. How does that sound to you, Chez?"

Preoccupied with what I suddenly saw, I quickly glanced from the two men who had separated from their third accomplice, back to the lone gunman who was in the process of raising a big chrome automatic. Unable to alert the men around me, I came up out of my seat with the hidden twin forty-fives. Having lost sight of the other two gunmen, I concentrated solely on the one as I let my guns go. Striking him square in the upper chest, I watched momentarily as his body crashed into the bar and slid to the floor. Turning to face my guest, I noticed the look of shock plastered upon his face at the same moment I saw the red dot on his forehead.

Diving towards Bocca, as he raised up out of the chair oblivious to the doom that awaited him, I hollered to Qwen, who was on his feet with two glocks in his hands. "Fire into the direction of the beam, nigga."

Making contact with Bocca, we careened into the table behind him. However, the burning sensation I felt in my shoulder was proof that not all the shots I'd heard had went astray. Bocca was safe, but I had taken one in his place.

Slowly making it to my feet, I saw Qwen and Carlos walking through the chaotic crowd of screaming people. Their weapons spit round after round into two jerking bodies. I wasn't sure, but from where I stood they looked like the partners of the lone gunman.

Grabbing me by my good arm, Bocca spoke in an alarming manner. "You're hurt, my friend! Come, Chez, we have to get out of here." Rushing through the crowd with Carlos and Qwen covering our exit, it was impossible for me not to know what Bocca was thinking.

The way he kept staring said it all; I had saved his life and our bond was now solidified.

Sipping my drink, I stared out the first class window of the plane, at the clouds that surrounded me. Even shot and bandaged, I concluded that our trip had been a success. Not even the numbing pain I felt in my shoulder could hinder my excitement. Just the mere thought of the twenty keys Bocca had gratefully fronted me instead of the planned ten, gave me a broader insight into the exceptional growth my crew would be experiencing real soon. Like he said, in no way had I ever imagined having this much power. But now that the stakes had been raised, I planned to take over the city and shit on all who had carried me in the process. Taking another sip of my drink, I just hoped that Qwen, Tara and Michelle made it home safely. Closing my eyes in thought, I decided that they would make it and once they did, I'd show the world that my time had come.

Chapter 9

With heavy, fluttering eyelids, I leaned back further into the comfort of Neeta's widespread legs as I sipped the remainder of my drink. The heat flowing from her center only added to the sweet feeling of her gently massaging fingers that were busy working every ounce of tension from my hard frame. Allowing the feeling of pure pleasure to take over, I closed my eyes in thought. If not for Qwen and his ability to hold the business together in my absence, spending the weekend with Neeta away from the stress of pagers and constant phone calls wouldn't be possible.

Smiling inwardly at how lucky I was to have him on my team, along with the realization that this woman had the magical fingers of a professional, I was immediately distraught when I felt Neeta release her grip on my shoulders. Giving me a peck on the neck, she rose to exit the Jacuzzi.

Turning in her direction, I selfishly questioned, "Where you think you're going woman? I know you don't think you're finished, do you?" Seriously wanting her to return to the task, I glared defiantly in her direction.

"If it's alright with you, I was going to refresh my drink." Sucking her teeth, she shook her head as she glared back towards me with hands on shapely hips. "Damn, baby. You're so spoiled at times." Switching across the room with water pouring from her naked frame, she winked over her shoulder, shooting a seductive smile my way.

No longer tired, the sight of Neeta's perfect, heart shaped ass swaying fluidly across the room grabbed my attention whole heartedly. The immediate return of tension that began to throb in my center was begging to be attended to all of a sudden. Smiling, I realized that she needed to massage that shit, and soon.

Watching my member get harder and harder, it dawned on me that no other woman had this kind of power over me. I never got tired of sexing Neeta. I loved making love to Monya, but not even her sex compared to the wild, uninhibited intercourse I experienced with Neeta. Thinking that Monya would more than likely kill the both of us if she had the slightest idea of what was going on, I heard Neeta's feet padding softly across the carpet.

Reaching the Jacuzzi, Neeta joked, "I'm back, spoiled brat. I brought you another drink too, baby." Placing the drink on the side of the Jacuzzi, her eyes widened at what she saw sticking out of the water. "Umph. Umph. Umph," she said, reaching down to grab the head. Running her hand up and down the considerable length, she licked her lips. "Damn, boo, what the hell were you doing while I was gone?"

Feeling her fist tighten in an upwards stroke, I closed my eyes a fraction of an inch and exhaled slowly. "I was thinking about your sexy ass," I groaned. "Put that damn drink down and get back in here, girl. You got business to attend to."

Placing her drink beside mine, on her way back in the water, Neeta eagerly replied, "Your wish is my command, cutie."

Grinning at her humor and the way she held tightly to my dick, I laughed, "Baby, do you plan to hold it the rest of the night or put it somewhere it can do some real good?"

Frowning playfully in response, she turned her back to me and slowly began to sit down on it, as I watched her swallow me inch by painstaking inch. Gasping for breath, Neeta swirled her hips in a slow rhythmic manner, while making her inner muscles grip and release me.

Clasping my eyes tightly together, I massaged her soft ass cheeks, while savoring the feel of her warm, pulsing insides. Each time Neeta raised her hips, it became more and more obvious why I was so crazy about her. It was the way she worked her inner muscles that had me gone.

Nearing her climax, Neeta leaned flush against my chest as she increased her movements. Becoming vocal, she pumped up and down harder while frantically tweaking her nipples. "You love this pussy, don't you? Huh, baby?" Whimpering loudly, she bit her lip in a state of half hysterical pleasure. "You're so big, baby. Oh...God... Chez! You're soooo...big!"

Rising up to meet her, stroke for stroke, I pumped back with a piston like urgency.

"You're damn right, I love this pussy!" I grunted through clenched teeth, feeling my toes curling up. Unsuccessful in my attempt at holding back, the combination of the tightness I was immersed in, and her loud moans sent me over the edge. Grabbing her hips, I slammed her body down on my own and shot my seed deep inside her.

Reaching a leg trembling orgasm at the force of the deep, hard invasion, Neeta yelled out, "Yes! Oh, yes, Chez!" before grinding down hard one last time and leaning her head backwards to kiss me long and hard.

Breaking our kiss, I wiped the sweat from her brow and wrapped my arms protectively around her. Listening to her rapid breathing as I felt her increased heartbeat, it suddenly became clear to me that I was beginning to catch feelings for the first time since Monya. That being the case, I was ready to give her the opportunity of receiving some of the benefits that came along with being my woman. I just hoped that she was aware that the level I was prepared to elevate her to wouldn't allow her an out. If she agreed to my proposal, it would undoubtedly be for keeps.

"Boom! Boom! Boom! Boom!, Boom! Boom! Boom! Boom! Tonight's the night that I plan my hit/ Yeah/ Deep cover on the incognito tip."

The crowd that surrounded the packed club turned their heads towards the approaching red Land Cruiser, that sported a gold grill and rims to match as "Deep Cover" blared from the speakers. Although the windows were tinted, the gawking crowd was aware that Qwen rode in the truck. And like the words of the song, it was widely known and well understood that anyone who got out of hand would also find themselves getting hit. Qwen's reputation as a gun-buster was legendary, and not even his time away had been able to deter that.

Frowning, Mann glared from the opposite side of the street. Watching the Land Cruiser park with the thunderous sounds beating from within, Mann turned to Dax and sneered, "Check this nigga out, rolling through here like he's a fucking Don or some shit!" Ice grilling, Mann argued, "He ain't shit. Fuck him!"

Sucking his toothpick, Dax shook his head in response. Choosing to stay quiet, Dax solemnly stared across the street as the occupants of the Land Cruiser exited the truck to the hungry looks of the women who immediately surrounded them.

Qwen, Dresser, Boo-Boo and Sam exited the truck, leaving the music on and doors open for the benefit of the numerous eyeballing spectators that lined the sidewalks. They immediately began to politic with the crowd. Knowing that they were ghetto superstars, the scantily dressed females who danced seductively around the truck in an attempt at garnering their attention was nothing new to any of them. They received this type of drama wherever they went in the city, so it was a normal occurrence.

Escaping the attentions of an overly anxious female, Boo-Boo stood off to the side of the truck and scanned through the faces of the vast crowd. Locking eyes with a pair that were already locked on him, Boo-Boo's facial features changed into an angry mask.

Hating the individual he now found himself in a silent battle of stares with, he mouthed the words, "What the fuck you looking at, nigga?" in Mann's direction.

Noticing the defiant, unblinking glare that Mann fixed on him, Boo-Boo held his arms out in a taunting manner, inviting him to come get some.

Seeing the exchange between Boo-Boo and Mann, Qwen excused himself from the young lady he was mackin' and patted Sam on the shoulder. "Yo, we may have a problem, bro."

Immediately getting his attention, they stepped to Boo-Boo. Staring across the street, Qwen asked, "What's going on, Boo-Boo?"

Refusing to break his stare, Boo-Boo grumbled, "I hate that nigga Mann, kid. There's nothing I want more than to bust his head, dog."

Balling his face up as he stared at Mann, Qwen gave him a silent look of warning. Although he didn't necessarily want to take it there with Mann's trouble making ass, Qwen knew him better than the rest of his young crew. Therefore, he was aware that if it did jump off, when it came to Mann, it was either kill or be killed. Mann was an old school murderer, so Qwen knew first hand that he played for keeps.

Breaking the stare, Mann erupted in laughter as he walked away, shaking his head. Never turning around, he knew that his young protégé, Dax, followed close behind him. Even though he laughed on the outside, inside he was seething. Chez had already become a thorn in his side, with the fearless bravado that he disrespectfully exhibited. Now, to make matters worse; Qwen, the only other individual Mann hated even more than Chez, had aligned himself with their crew. At this point, Mann had no unrealistic expectations of conquering the two of them together, by himself. Needing assistance and having no other alternative, it suddenly became clear to him what his course of action would be.

"Look at all that ass waiting for us over there," Qwen commented in an attempt at taking Boo-Boo's attention off of Mann. "Come on, my nigga, we came out here to have some fun." Sighing at the angry look still on Boo-Boo's face, Qwen said, "He don't want any drama for real man. Believe me, partner, if he ever gets out of hand, we'll show him and his crew how we do things."

"Let's get the party started then," Boo-Boo replied, giving Qwen a pound.

Mann wasn't worth messing up what he could see had the makings of becoming a good night for them. Realizing that Qwen was right, Boo-Boo stared in the direction Mann had departed in one last time, before turning to follow Qwen and Sam back to the truck.

Thinking that there could never be a better time than the present to put my plan in action, I continued strolling hand in hand with Neeta. The waves crashed around us, while the stars shone brightly on the ocean's surface. Racking my brain for the best way to attack the issue, I came to the conclusion that there was no better way than to go directly at her. Halting in mid step, I pulled Neeta into my arms and kissed her softly.

Slowly pulling away, Neeta grinned, "Damn, baby, what did I do to deserve that…"

"Neeta, you know I'm feeling you a whole lot, right?" I questioned, cutting her words short.

"Of course, I know that, baby." Wrapping her arms around my neck, she stared deep into my eyes. "I'm feeling you more, though," Neeta smiled sweetly.

Wanting her to understand the seriousness of my words, I spoke slowly, while staring into her pretty brown eyes. "Here's the deal, baby. You already know I've got a woman, and I'm not even about to front like that's gonna change any time soon. But, I guess what I'm trying to say is, I want you to be my woman also."

Frowning with a slight hint of amusement mixed in, Neeta leaned her frame in closer to my own. "Now, I know I'm not the smartest bitch in the world, but how about you enlighten me on how you plan to work that out, baby."

Placing a finger over her lips, I said, "Shhh. Just listen to what I have to say. If you're not with it afterwards, I'll respect your position, alright?"

Shaking her head in acknowledgment of my words, she affectionately rubbed my head as she awaited an explanation.

Running my fingers through her long tresses, I allowed my thoughts to flow to the surface. "I want to be with you, Neeta. For as long as I can remember, I've wanted you. And now that you're in my life, I want nothing but the best for you. The only problem is, selfishly, I refuse to invest in you unless I'm positive that no other man besides me will have you."

Releasing her hold on my neck, Neeta snapped, "What? Nigga,

you're already the only motherfucking man in my life. Damn, Chez, what more do I have to do to show you I love you?" Dripping with attitude, she awaited an answer.

Smiling at her defiant display, I pulled her body back against mine. "Chill, ma. Damn! A nigga can't even talk to your evil ass," I joked. Seeing a smile creep back onto her still pouting face, I continued, "Baby, are you willing to only be with me, even if it means having to share me with Monya?"

"Hell, yeah!" she instantly replied. "You should have already known that, boo. But since you seem not to know where we really stand, let me pull your coat to something else." Giving me a no-nonsense look, she informed, "You better not let me catch you out there cheating either. I'm not playing, Chez. If you really want me to be your woman, then I'm laying claim to your ass as well. If you slip, I swear I'm gonna show you how I carry it about mine."

"I got you, baby. We're on the same page," I laughed. "Now, since I can't have my lady living below grade, the first thing we need to do is get rid of that Honda and find you a house..."

Jumping into my arms, Neeta cut me off. "Oh, I love you, Chez. Where can I look for my house at? And can I get a Lexus, boo?"

"You can get a Lexus, and you're welcome to search wherever you like for your house," I grinned.

I was doing better than I could have ever dreamed possible, since linking up with Bocca. In fact, thanks to him and the forty keys he was now fronting me each time, I was rich enough to allow ten women just like Neeta to purchase whips and houses at my expense.

Squealing excitedly, Neeta buried her head in my chest, before blurting out, "Thanks, Chez. I love you."

Hugging her tightly, I smiled at the excitement she expressed. I hoped she knew that at this point, there was no turning back. I had given her the chance to decide how she wanted to carry it. After making her choice, whether she realized it or not, I would murder her if she fucked up. Grinning slyly, the thought dawned on me that Neeta had just sold her soul to the devil.

Cradling the phone against his ear, Mann pulled away from the curb into the flow of traffic. Anxiously tapping on the steering wheel, he blanked out everything else around him, but the sound of the ringing phone.

"Yeah, who this?" the voice on the other end of the phone questioned.

"It's me, motherfucker! What's up?" Mann chuckled, instantly recognizing the voice.

"Ain't shit happening on this end, son. I should be the one asking you what's poppin', being that you never seem to get at your peep's these days, cuz."

"Yeah. Yeah. I know, nigga. But I'm here now, though. Where's Unique and Rio at?" Mann eagerly questioned.

"It's Mann," Supreme mumbled. "My bad, son. That's them niggas in the background. Anyway, holler at me. I get the feeling that this isn't just a normal family call, so what's going on down there in Virginia, cuz?"

Exhaling, Mann got straight to the point. "I got a few clown ass niggas down here who need to get dealt with, Supreme. I would feel much better if I had my family down here to back me up." Knowing they would come regardless, Mann decided to sweeten the deal for the hell of it. "We can kill two birds with one stone, cuz. The niggas are caked up, so we can get them and their dough. Afterwards, we'll just muscle our way right into their business, you feel me?"

"Oh, yeah. It's like that, huh?" Rambling on, Supreme stated, "You already know we're wit that, fam. Niggas are in for a rude awakening when we get there," he boasted. "Yo, we'll be down there tomorrow with mad product and more weapons than you're ready for, alright!"

"That's what's up," Mann replied, with a smug grin pasted on his face. "I can't wait to see you, nigga."

"Go to sleep then, cause when you wake up, I'll be in your damn face." Laughing, Supreme said, "I'm out, fam."

Hearing the phone go dead, Mann closed his phone and turned to Dax. "It's about to set the fuck off, Dax." Laughing triumphantly, he reached over and turned the music up as high as it would go.

Expressionless, Dax cradled his weapon and looked out the window, in deep thought.

Ready to set it off whenever and wherever, it didn't really matter to him whether Mann's New York people came down to assist or not. Not one to love, respect or fear any nigga, Dax had never really harbored any feelings toward Chez one way or the other.

Even though they happened to be rivals, Dax knew that like himself, Chez was a killer who got money by any means and feared no one. He had no doubt that Chez was real, but real or not, nothing would stop Dax from seeing him when the time came. Nothing. The wheels of destiny had already begun to turn, and with them, the lives of many would never be the same.

Chapter 10

After dropping Neeta off at home, I jumped back on the highway, turned my cell phone back on, and activated the cruise control on the Mercedes. Leaning back in the seat, I felt refreshed from our little vacation. Nevertheless, the weekend was over and the reality of the situation made it clear that it was time to pick up where I had left off. Business called. Popping my Tupac tape in, I picked the phone up and began punching in my home numbers. After not contacting Monya in over 48 hours, I figured I had better let her know I was back in the city.

Cradling the phone between my ear and shoulder, I listened to the ringing, while subconsciously thinking that I had been messing up bad lately. Between running the streets on a constant paper chase, the partying and putting in overtime with Neeta, I had been basically neglecting Monya and my daughter. Monya's voicemail picked up and I left her a sweet message. Ending the call, I made a mental note to get it together. I had come entirely too far to lose my original goal. I knew that before anything else, my reason for sacrificing in the streets was supposed to be for the security and happiness of my two favorite girls, not myself. Feeling the vibration in my lap, I cancelled the thoughts I had been having and reached for the phone.

"Yeah," I spoke into the receiver, only to have my ear assaulted by blaring music as a response.

Hollering over the music, Qwen questioned, "What's up, lil bro? I see you decided to come home, nigga."

"Yo, turn that shit down, man. I'm not trying to talk over all that bass," I sharply stated.

"Alright, hold on." Lowering the volume, he returned. "Okay, I said, I see you decided to bring your red ass home," he laughed.

"If I could trust you to handle the show for more than a weekend without fucking everything up, I would have gladly stayed away longer."

"Oh yeah," he laughed. "Nigga, you know I got this. Your ass could have stayed gone forever. But we both know why you really ran home. You're scared of Monya, nigga."

Sharing a hearty laugh at my expense, I got serious. "Has everything been flowing smoothly since I've been gone, player?"

"You know we're good, man. Everything is moving along according to plans."

Hearing the words, "Everything is going according to plans," brought the thought to mind that the last few months had been too trouble- free. We were seeing too much money for no one to be trying their hands in our direction. Niggas were hungry in the city, and no matter how hard we were prepared to go for ours, someone else out there was prepared to go just as hard or harder. Refusing to get caught slipping, I decided not to allow myself to get too comfortable. Letting the thought pass, I asked, "Where you at, my nigga?"

"I'm out, Lee Park, man. The whole crew is out here, and believe me when I tell you, there are too many bitches out here, kid. They're on our dicks hard, dog." Chuckling, he boasted, "Even though I've hit most of them, I'm willing to hold it down for you out here, until you arrive."

"Yeah, I have no doubt that you will." I smiled to myself, thinking that no one I knew loved flossing and showing off more than he did. "Look here, bro, I'm gonna shoot to the crib for a quick shower and change of clothes, then I'll be on my way. Stay put, alright?"

"Yo, hold up, Chez." Raising his voice, Qwen commanded, "Pull that mother-fucking car over, girl. Where the fuck have you been...? Better yet, don't say shit, just sit your ass still until I finish this call!" Sighing heatedly, he said, "I'm back, bro. These females don't seem to realize that I'm running the show, not them."

"You know you're nuts, don't you?" I laughed. Handle your women then, nigga. Just don't be out there acting a fool. I'll see you in a little while." Hanging up, I shook my head at the antics of my friend.

Arriving at the security gate of my housing community, I placed the allotted identification card in the scanner slot and watched as the steel gates slid open to grant my access.

Smiling, it never ceased to amaze me that my community was guarded day and night from the same type of criminal element that I personified.

Reaching my house, I cruised up the long circular driveway and hit the remote mounted on the dash. Slowly, the doors to my three car garage began to lift, displaying my Q45 and the pride of my small fleet, an 840 BMW. Seeing that Monya's G.S. wasn't there confirmed that she wasn't home. This fit perfectly into my plans, because now I could get right and bounce without a confrontation.

Closing the garage doors, I exited the Benz and entered the house. The house was new, and even though I hadn't really been there enough to break it in, it felt good to be home. Strolling across the Italian marble floor, I was still in awe of its beauty. From the fountain that sat in the center of the foyer, to the three story horseshoe staircase that sported a clear, skylight ceiling; I still found it hard to believe that I actually lived here.

Thinking of what the purchase of my little slice of heaven had set me back as I ascended the steps, I realized that some serious strings had been pulled to make this particular dream a reality. At a price tag of nine-hundred and eighty thousand, I had spent a bundle, not to mention the cost of furnishings. They say that success is non-existent in the ghetto, but I was proud to be one ex-stick-up man and petty hustler who had truly made it.

Entering our third floor master bedroom, I strolled straight through to the large doors that opened to the balcony. Inhaling the fresh air that came off the river, I marveled at the view before me. Noticing that our boat dock was the only one that sat empty, I made a mental note to purchase one as soon as I found time to do so.

Glancing at my watch, it dawned on me that I needed to get a move on. I had people awaiting my arrival, and the only thing that stood between us was a shower and a change of clothes. Turning to go back in the house, I actually felt that nothing could stop me. In my mind, I was the man.

Staring at the approaching Range Rover, Mann couldn't help the extra dose of power that he suddenly felt. Now that his cousins had arrived, he realized that between them and his crew, no one could stop them from easily taking over the city. With arms folded across his chest, Mann silently eyed the vehicle as it came to an abrupt stop before him.

Stepping from the truck first, Unique winked conspiratorially at his cousin with a sly grin plastered upon his mocha complexioned face, before reaching a hand out to grasp Mann's.

"Yeah, nigga, you thought I wasn't gonna make the party, " Rio coolly spat with a smirk in place, as he exited the Range close behind his brother.

Giving his cousin a firm handshake, Mann replied, "You miss a party? Please. Nigga, I knew you were coming." Releasing his hand, Mann had to blink with the realization that Unique and Rio could pass for twins. With the same height, muscular builds and rugged, thugged out demeanor, they were identical in appearance. Jarred out of his thoughts at the sight of Supreme making his exit from the truck, Mann was unable to disguise the smile that lit up his face.

"Damn! I was wondering if you were planning to get up out that shit, nigga."

Hugging Mann, Supreme whispered through the clenched diamond encrusted gold teeth that were clamped tightly around the toothpick in the corner of his slightly smirking mouth, "You already know the best must always be saved for last, pimp."

Grinning at Supreme's reply, Mann stared appreciatively at the diamonds that covered Supreme's neck, wrists, fingers and teeth. In a mocking tone, Mann questioned, "Did you come down here to help me deal with these niggas, or pull their bitches with all that shine on?"

"I may do a little bit of both, cuz. It depends on how bad their bitches are," he concluded. "Anyway, at the moment, my mission is to deal with the niggas, so tell me what we're up against."

Snubbing his nose in a stink manner, Mann said, "The head nigga in their crew is a nigga name Chez."

The bitterness was evident in his tone when he continued. "Qwen is next in line. Then you have Boo-Boo, Sam, Dresser and Satin. With the exception of Satin, who smokes these days, and Dresser's soft ass, the rest of their crew are on some shoot first and ask questions later shit."

Shaking his head in understanding, Supreme gave Mann a quizzical look. "Are they the only ones we have to worry about?"

"Yeah" Lying through his teeth, Mann broke their previous eye contact. "It's only the ones I told you about, cuz."

Only thing was, he purposely withheld the fact that over two hundred 3rd Ward soldiers would gladly follow Chez's lead if they were called upon to do so.

Eyeing Mann closely, Supreme had a feeling that his cousin wasn't keeping it real, but before he jumped headfirst into any situation he always took the time to investigate. This situation would be no different, so he had no doubt that he would soon find out everything he needed to know and more. Sighing lightly, Supreme grinned devilishly, "Enough talking then, nigga. I need to get a look at what we're up against, so let's go see if we can find these clowns."

Following his peeps back to the truck, Mann's features were set in an ice grill as he contemplated bringing Chez and his crew down. Having his family by his side was the determining factor that he knew would soon lead to the demise of his enemies. With their renowned murder game and his crew of gun busters, Mann anxiously thought that it was only a matter of time until he held the power that belonged to him and him only.

Whipping through traffic in my money green and gold Yamaha FZR750, I couldn't describe the feeling I was experiencing. If I had to pick one word to define it, I'd say that I felt invincible. In my mind, I owned the streets when I sped through them on my baby.

Navigating the sleek machine through the traffic that was backed up for blocks in every direction around the park, I was able to cruise through the entrance without any real effort. Slowing my speed, as

I removed my helmet and donned a pair of Gucci frames, I peered through the crowd in search of my crew who would undoubtedly be carrying it like celebrities. Seeing my crew, I sprayed rocks in my wake as I spun tires, heading in their direction.

Reaching my destination, I was far from surprised to find that the 3rd Ward was out in vast numbers. That's how we rolled. And even though I saw fifty or more crowded around, I was aware that many more roamed through the park. Acknowledging my people as I stepped off the bike, I made my way through the crowd to where I noticed Qwen talking to two dimepieces.

Licking my lips invitingly as I caught the eyes of the too thick, light complexioned cutie, who left no doubt about the fact that she too liked what she saw by the manner that she seductively stared back.

" I see you're doing real well for yourself, bro."

Breaking the magnetic eye contact I had been sharing with Ms. Delicious, I shot my man a questioning look as I approached.

Rising up from the hood of the Beamer, Qwen reached out to give me a pound. Talking to no one in particular, he said, "I knew his ass would get here in no time flat." Steering me towards the women, he stated, "Toshia and Monique, this here is my man, Chez. Chez, meet Monique and Toshia."

Immediately taking charge, Monique reached out to grasp my hand, then in the sweetest voice I had ever heard, she said, "I'm glad to finally meet you, Chez. I've heard of you forever," she stated, giving me her picture perfect smile.

Holding onto her soft hand, I concluded that even though I hadn't heard anything about her prior to our meeting, I too was more than happy to be making her acquaintance. Eyeing her with obvious appreciation, I countered, "Where have you been hiding, and how is it possible that I haven't seen you before?" with a raised brow.

Giggling in a low, sultry manner, she replied, "I've been around. Only, I don't make it a habit of frequenting any of the more dangerous spots where I'm sure you hang." Suddenly slipping her hand from my grasp, Monique flashed a dry smile, before adding, "Anyway, my man keeps me in the house where he's able to monitor me as closely as possible."

Scanning her frame admiringly, I slowly shook my head in understanding, before replying, "I can't say I blame him." Deciding immediately that whoever her man was had to be slipping in his game if she was here verbally battling with me, I asked, "Where is this so-called man of yours now?"

Dropping her eyes, she responded with an unsteady voice. "He's locked up, and after a month of just sitting around the house doing nothing, I'm tired. This little outing was a pleasant change of pace, after the boredom I've had to suffer through."

Deciding on the spot that she was more than likely just as horny as she was bored, I figured I'd make a play for some ass. As far as I was concerned, she was bound to give the pussy away, sooner or later, so I may as well be the one to receive it now. "This isn't a real cure for boredom," I informed, flashing a phony smile. "How about the four of us get together later and puff a few L's, have some drinks and then grab dinner?"

Chewing on her succulent lip in thought, she cut her eyes in Toshia's direction before glancing back at me and innocently responding, "I don't know, Chez."

Seeing the apparent indecision pasted on her face, the last thing I was prepared to allow her was an easy out. Playing my ace card, I hunched my shoulders in a nonchalant manner, peered off into the crowd, then coolly stated, "Look, Monique. If you would rather sit around the house bored to death, don't let me stop you. Only, I'm sure that what I have planned will be a whole lot more fun, because I'll be getting my party on regardless of whether you come along or not." Staring directly into her eyes as I spoke, I insisted, "I have no ulterior motives. There are no strings attached, at all. I would just like to help you unwind, while getting to know you better."

Giving her my boyish smile, which dripped with charm, I wanted to laugh at the truth of my last statement. Because if I had my way, I'd be getting to know her a whole lot better before the end of the night.

Pausing as if to weigh her decision, Monique whispered sexily, "Since you put it that way, I guess I can roll with ya'll."

"Psst," Shaking her head in disgust, Toshia snapped in a high pitched tone, "You two are true works of art. First, you flat out ignore us. Then you have the nerve to make a motherfucking date, including the two of us, without even asking if we want to go." Sucking her teeth, she blurted out, "You two don't have any damn manners."

Pulling her close, Qwen said, "As long as the smoke, drink and dinner are free, you know your ass will be there. So, you may as well chill with all that noise, shorty."

Laughing at his words, I had to do a double take at the sexy pout Toshia shot my way, followed by what I thought was a blatant show of jealousy when she rolled her eyes. Momentarily locking eyes, I immediately became aware that she too wanted my attention. Coolly allowing my eyes to pass over every inch of her delightful curves, I concluded that behind her feisty attitude lied a sexual wildcat. Giving her a sly wink, I turned to Monique with a smirk in place. However, the thought traveled through my mind that when the time came, Toshia's body would no doubt be something special as well.

Needing to politic with a few of my soldiers who I had glimpsed on my journey through the park, I arrogantly stated, "I look forward to seeing you tonight, ma, but right now I've got people to see."

Beginning to walk off, I tossed the words over my shoulder, "Wear something sexy." With a cheesy smile in place, I knew that she was far from ready for what I had in store for her tonight.

Chez was fine as hell, and a gangster to match. Watching him walk away, Monique had a devious smirk plastered on her face as her mind worked rapidly. She could barely tear her eyes away from his slowly disappearing form, before thoughts came to mind of just how sweet being his woman could be. Having already heard rumors of how enormous his thing was, the fact that he was sexy as hell, paid, and feared in the streets only added to his attraction.

Unconsciously allowing a slight giggle to escape her beautiful lips, she concluded that he had no idea what he was getting himself into, flirting with her. Making up her mind that Chez would undoubtedly receive every drop of her goodies before the end of the night, Monique rationalized that his little so-called game had nothing to do with her decision. If there was any game involved, it would belong to her. Confident in the knowledge that he had met his match with her, Monique defiantly pondered the fact that all the chicks he now had were in trouble.

Turning to face Qwen and Toshia with a devilish grin pasted on her face, Monique had no doubt that tonight would be the beginning of much more than dinner, smoke and drinks.

Tonight she planned to work her magic.

Chapter 11

"Snap the hell out of that daze, girl. What in the world are you sitting there thinking about? You've been out in space for the longest time."

Startled, Monya snapped out of her haze and focused her attention back on her girl. Giving her a phony smile, she said, "It's nothing, girl. Never mind me."

Unconsciously allowing her attention to wander back into the packed park, she searched for Chez's silhouette once more.

From the first moment she had witnessed him entering the park, she hadn't allowed him to disappear from her view. That being the case, Monya was well aware of the interaction that he and his newest hoochie had just shared. The mixture of sadness and jealously that suddenly weighed heavily upon her was unexplainable. Although in her mind, she was well aware that she shared her man with many women, to see the display of lust with her own eyes was too much for her. Brokenhearted, she inwardly screamed When will it all end? And, Why do I put up with the shit in the first place? Though this wasn't the first time she'd had those thoughts, at that moment, Monya really wondered why she didn't have someone else on the side as well.

Suddenly realizing how quiet it had gotten in the car, she slowly swiveled to face Yaya, only to find her glaring contemptuously back with an agitated look on her face.

"Damn! Why you all in my grill, bitch?" Monya blurted, with an uneasy giggle.

Rolling her eyes, Yaya sighed and said, "I don't know what's gotten into you, but you're trippin'." In a whiny voice she confirmed, "you're not enjoying yourself, nor am I. So, if this is how it's gonna be, you can just take me home."

Exhaling, Monya rolled her eyes in response to Yaya's statement. As far as she was concerned, the day couldn't get any worse, so taking Yaya home was more than likely a good idea. Deciding that she wasn't hardly feeling the park any longer either, she admitted, "You're right, girl. I'm not good company right now, so I think I'm gonna go on home myself."

"Umm-hmm," Yaya mumbled in reply as she leaned her seat further back and turned her head angrily towards the passenger window.

Ignoring Yaya's antics, Monya raised the volume on her set and glanced across the park in an attempt to catch one last glimpse of Chez as she pulled off.

"Bomp! Bomp!"

"Monya, watch out, girl!" Yaya yelled out.

Slamming down on the brake pedal, Monya nervously snapped back to attention.

"Girl, you almost hit that pretty ass Range Rover!"

Somewhat shaken, Monya placed the Lexus back in park, and allowed her heart rate to calm down. Glancing towards the black

Range, she silently stared as the driver's window slowly began to lower. As if in slow motion, the occupants safely disguised on the other side of the tint came into view. Instead of slowing down, her heartbeat increased even more at the initial sight of the driver. Before the thought of who he was could completely enter her mind, she stared through unblinking eyes as he slowly opened his mouth. The diamond-encrusted fronts that glimmered brightly before her eyes left no doubt that whoever he was, his dough was plentiful.

"You alright, ma?" Supreme asked, holding eye contact.

Instantly getting goose bumps from his deep, sexy voice, Monya stammered as she too held his stare, "Uh… yeah. I'm… fine."

"You look a little shook, ma. Are you sure you're alright?" he asked, thinking that she looked just fine. In all actuality, he was betting that she was the finest female he had seen since coming to town.

Nervously glancing around to make certain that they hadn't made a scene, Monya unconvincingly replied, "No… I mean, yes!" She blushed. "I'm really alright…"

She allowed her words to trail off, thinking to herself that she needed to get going before Chez's crazy ass caught wind of her talking to a nigga in a Range. Attempting to avert her eyes from the seductive stare that seemed to bore through her, she bit down on her bottom lip to control her blushing.

"I'm sorry for almost hitting you."

"It's all good, ma," Supreme sincerely replied. "If that's what it took for me to meet you, then it would have been worth it." Smirking, he humorously added, "If I'm lucky, maybe you will almost run into me again while I'm in town. Be safe, and I look forward to our next meeting, love." Winking his eye conspiratorially, he hit the power button to raise the window, and pulled off.

Unable to reply, Monya watched with her mouth partially open in awe as the Range cruised further into the park. Although it was unlike her to be interested in anyone besides Chez, right now her thoughts were riveted on the stranger who had just exited her life as fast as he had entered it.

Glancing through the rearview mirror while making his exit, Supreme displayed no emotion to his cousins. But in all truth, he wasn't as unfazed by the little meeting that had just transpired as he would have had them believe. Realizing that he may have just played himself by not making a proper introduction, he found it hard to run his little uninterested ploy with her for some reason.

"Umph, umph, umph!" Mann chuckled, shaking his head at his cousin.

"What?" Supreme asked, diverting his attention from the rearview mirror and the Lexus reflected in it, back to Mann.

Patting his cousin on the shoulder, Mann said, "You know you're that nigga, right?"

"Huh?" Supreme asked, not quite understanding where Mann was going with the conversation.

"Man, you haven't even been in the city a whole hour, and already you've met and left a lasting impression upon dude's girl."

"Dude's girl? What dude?" Supreme snapped, baffled.

"Chez, nigga! You just macked on his bitch," Mann confirmed with a smile pasted on his features.

"Oh, yeah," Supreme stated, more so to himself than anyone else. Thinking that she was a certified star from what he was able to see of her, he had to admit that if nothing else, he was already aware that the nigga had good taste. To Mann he said, "I plan to do a lot more than mack on her in that case."

"I can't say that I blame you, fam. But for the record, don't lose sight of why you're really here, alright?" Mann smugly remarked.

Giving Mann a blank expression, he said, "I could never do that, cuz."

Mann had no idea that Supreme had his own agenda that no one was aware of. When Mann had called him, he had unknowingly set events in motion that not even he could have imagined.

"Umph!" Yaya loudly exclaimed. "Did you see how fine that nigga was? Not to mention that expensive, beautiful truck he was driving. It only added insults to the rest of the whips in the park."

"He was alright."

Monya had been impressed, although she didn't want her girl to know it, even now she was replaying his looks over and over in her mind.

"Alright my ass! That nigga was the shit, and you know it, bitch!" Giving Monya a quizzical glare, she stated, "You also know the nigga was feeling you, so what are you gonna do when you see him again?"

"I'm not gonna do shit! You and everyone else in this city know that I got a man, so stop talking foolish!"

"Whatever, girl!" Yaya arrogantly replied with a mischievous grin in place as she focused her attention on her meticulously done manicure. "I'm just saying, man or not, ain't a damn thing wrong with having a little extra on the side for those lonely nights." Cutting her eyes at Monya, she informed, "You're already aware that every bitch in town is chasing Chez, trying to give up the ass. Psst! There's no reason why you shouldn't be getting yours too."

Realizing that Yaya was right, especially after the long distance episode that she had just witnessed, there was no response needed.

Suddenly stressed out, Monya turned the music up and pulled out into traffic. Deaf to the sounds blaring from the speakers, all that she could hear was an inner voice screaming, Chez is no longer handling his business where you are concerned. From the looks of it, he was too busy being caught by the hordes of bitches who are constantly chasing him.

Loving him with all her heart and soul, she concluded that two wrongs could never equal to one right. So for the moment, she would continue to hold him down. Yet, it was becoming more and more apparent to her, that sooner or later, if he didn't tighten up, she would have to find another to scratch the itch that burned within her.

"Hey, Chez!"

Turning in the direction of the sultry voice, I said, "Hey, cutie!" and kept it moving.

Winking my eye at another group of scantily dressed shorties who pranced by with the bottoms of their cheeks escaping from their tiny shorts, I grinned lustfully as they put extra twists in their already shimmying hips for my benefit.

Shaking my head, I continued to politic with members of my crew as we strolled through the packed park. Although I was surrounded by a crowd of festive individuals as usual, my mind was focused on business.

With my attention riveted on the group assembled near me, I was caught off guard when I heard a familiar voice whisper in my ear, "You love all the attention you're receiving out this bitch, don't you, nigga?" Chuckling in a low tone, Boo-Boo answered his own question. "Hell yeah, you love it. You fake motherfucker!"

Turning my head to give my dog a pound, I smirked and said, "Whatever, nigga! You know I've been the center of attention for years. On the real, whether you've noticed it or not, there's a lot of ass kissing being thrown in your direction as well."

Before Boo-Boo could respond, a thick red dime-piece in a pair of jean shorts that looked like they had been painted on, walked behind him. Whispering something in his ear, she placed a piece of paper in his hand and sexily sashayed away.

Turning towards me once again, he hunched his shoulders in a 'What can I say?' fashion, and shot me a silly grin. "Point proven!" I teased, laughing along with the remainder of our steadily growing group.

Grabbing Boo-Boo's shoulders in a cheerful manner, I began to lead our procession back on an aimless trek through the park.

Feeling on top of the world, I came to the realization that although my crew and I had been popular before, it was astounding just how much our popularity had grown since our paper had increased. With forty keys flowing through our hands each week, it was only natural that the city and everyone in it would bow down. Smiling inwardly, I decided that I wouldn't have it any other way.

"There they are, right there!" Mann excitedly stated, pointing up ahead.

"They who? Where?" Unique grunted in a high-pitched tone. "There are a bunch of niggas out there, cuz."

"Right there, with the velour sweatsuits on, surrounded by dudes," Mann snapped hastily. "You can't miss them, with those big ass chains they got on."

Pointing up ahead as well, Rio cut in, "One is dark-skinned, and the light-complexioned one has his arm draped over dude's shoulder."

"Yeah, I see them now," Supreme coolly stated. "If I'm going to be fucking his bitch when we kill him, how about you tell me which one is the kid Chez, Mann."

"He's the one with the red sweatsuit and gold shades on, "Mann confirmed. " I hate that fronting ass nigga!" he angrily spat with a mean mug plastered on his face that left no doubt that he meant exactly what he said.

Chuckling, Supreme casually replied, "Ease up, cousin. You'll have your chance to deal with money. Be patient. He'll get his."

Cruising up slowly, the tinted black Range that sported chrome rims, New York plates and sounds furiously beating out of the interior, immediately caught the attention of me and my crew of gun toting soldiers that surrounded him as it came to an abrupt stop.

Unable to see inside, but straining my eyes to do so nonetheless, I could feel the sudden change taking place around me. At that moment, the back window on the passenger side began to lower, along with my frown at the face that came into view.

"Well, well! If it ain't the king of the 3rd Ward himself!" Mann tauntingly remarked with bitterness apparent in his eyes and tone of voice.

Reaching an arm out to refrain Boo-Boo's forward movement, I felt the muscles in my own body tense. "Cut the games, nigga. I don't fuck with you and you know it, so keep it moving!" I venomously stated.

Laughing loud and boisterously, Mann spat, "Apparently someone has given you the idea that you're running shit around here for real, young nigga." Popping his door and stepping from the truck, he defiantly sneered in the faces of Chez's crew, then barked, "Fuck you, and fuck the rest of you niggas!"

Before Mann's words were completely out of his mouth, the sounds of weapons being drawn and the scurrying feet of the crowd that had gathered around the melee could be heard.

"Put your weapons away!" I shouted.

Enraged, I glared at Mann as he confidently returned my look with one that was just as cold and hard. Realizing that the time to deal with him had arrived, I removed my jacket, jewelry and glasses. Reaching towards the small of my back, I discarded my weapon as well. Handing everything to Boo-Boo, I caught the glimmer of excitement in his eyes as I turned back to Mann. In a zone, I growled as I moved in a low crouch towards him.

"Let me know it's really like that, nigga!"

"Yeah, that's what I'm talking about!" he countered, moving towards me with a broad grin in place. "Let's do this then, youngster!"

Watching his stance with unblinking eyes, I quickly became aware that he hadn't been born with a gun in his hand after all. The nigga was confident for a reason. He actually had hands, I thought as I barely avoided a lightening-quick two piece before landing a bone crushing body blow of my own.

113

Tensing slightly at the force of the punch, Mann smugly informed, "That's what I'm talking about, punk! Now, it's my turn!"

He faked a right while shuffling inside so quickly, that the left-right combination he threw caught me completely by surprise.

"Ahh!" the crowd roared as I stumbled backwards in an attempt to stay on my feet.

Shaking my head to clear the haze, I caught a glimpse of Boo-Boo raising my four-fifth towards Mann's head.

"Boo-Boo, no!" I angrily declared in a forceful tone.

Lowering the weapon with an ice grill in my direction, we momentarily locked eyes in a silent battle.

The sound of a familiar voice humorously stating, "That shit there had to hurt, bro," awakened me. Winking his eye, Qwen instructed, "Whip his ass, Chez! He can't see you, bro!"

Raising my hands, I paraded back in.

Watching from the confines of the truck, Supreme lowered the weapon that had been trained on Boo-Boo. Thanks to the kid Chez, his man's life had been spared. Refusing to expose his hand and give up the element of surprise, he had chosen to remain out of sight and allow the initial drama to play out while he became aware of the opposition. Concluding that he hadn't traveled down 95 South to fight, Supreme figured that the enemy didn't need to know of his existence until the bodies were ready to drop.

Deciding on the spot, that Mann was in no way ready to control the show once his so-called enemies were dealt with, Supreme realized that he would have to make sure that sole control was granted to him instead.

Focusing his attention back on the combatants, he inwardly grinned as the crowd roared at the series of combinations that Chez landed into Mann's rapidly swelling face. Winking at the staggering blow that left a dumbfounded look on Mann's face right before it smacked into the dirt, Supreme shook his head. At this rate, he knew that taking over his cousin's rule would be the easiest task that he ever embarked upon.

Standing over Mann's prone form, I contemplated stomping the shit out of him, but decided against it. I had already made my point. I had to give it to him; his hands were swift as hell. Staring down, it was crystal clear to me, everyone else and him—whenever he woke up—that my hands were better.

Walking off as niggas exited the truck to retrieve Mann's unconscious form, I was met by Qwen, Boo-Boo and Sam. With smiles plastered on their faces, the jokes began.

"I thought you were done for when you stood still and allowed him to catch you with that three-piece," Boo-Boo admitted. "Before I let you take a loss to that clown, I figured I would go ahead and murder his ass."

Chuckling along with Sam, who was nodding his head in agreement, I countered, "The last thing you needed to do was catch a body in front of all these people. Plus, if you would have killed him, you wouldn't have had the chance to see me knock his ass out."

"You got a point," Boo-Boo stated nonchalantly.

It was Qwen's words that really struck a chord in my mind. "Before it's over, you may just wish that you killed him after all, bro.

The worst thing you could have ever done was whip him in front of all these people, then give his crazy ass a chance to come back."

Sighing lowly, I was no longer laughing as I had to agree with him. Mann was far from your average hood. He wasn't about to take his ass whipping sitting down. In the back of my mind, I was aware that from this point on, I would have to keep my eyes wide open.

Nevertheless, like any other obstacle that had ever been placed before me, if it was going down, I would have no problem getting it over with. For now, I had other more important things in mind. Tonight, I had a date with Monique, and nothing besides that was worthy of commanding my thoughts.

For some reason, Monya was acting strange. She seemed distant and unhappy. Chalking it up to the fact that I probably needed to spend a little more time at home with her and my daughter, I planned to do just that, soon. Only tonight, I had a date and no intentions on missing it.

After playing with my daughter, I jumped in the shower and got dressed. Feeling fresh, but looking even fresher, I gave myself a once over in the mirror before grabbing my gun off the dresser. Just in case I ran into a problem, I figured that I would much rather be safe than sorry.

Turning at the sound of approaching footsteps, I came face to face with my boo. Winking my eye slyly, I gave her a cheerful grin and silently awaited her usual blushing response.

Stopping in the doorway and leaning against the frame, Monya sighed as if she carried the weight of the world on her shoulders. Speaking in a low whisper, she asked, "Where are you going, Chez?" Her eyes traveled questioningly down my frame.

Caught off guard, and somewhat surprised, I stared at her with my brow raised in an annoyed manner. "I'm going out," I replied, wondering why after all this time, she was suddenly questioning my whereabouts.

"Out, huh!" she laughed sarcastically. "Oh yeah?" Speaking with a tone that was slow, but dripping with a mixture of bitterness and frustration, she stated, "You're on your way out again, and I haven't seen you once all weekend."

Becoming more annoyed by the moment, I turned back towards the mirror and flatly countered, "That's right. I'm going out. I had business to take care of this weekend, and just because I'm back, don't mean that the shit stops."

"I see," Monya informed me with a trace of tears evident in her eyes. "It seems that business always comes first these days. Even with this big house, all the luxury vehicles and more money than we could have ever dreamed of, what I want the most is you. Only thing is, that's not possible, because suddenly you're further out of my reach now than before we got all this." Unable to halt the tears that ran down her smooth almond-colored cheeks, her voice trembled when she added, "Sometimes I feel like we were better off before all this, Chez."

Staring at her through the mirror, the only thought that came to mind was that she had to be crazy. Unlike her, I was better just the way I was. Frowning, I exhaled.

"You're trippin', Monya. Look how far we've come." Turning to face her, I pleaded, "Give me a minute, baby. In a little while I'll have everything in order. I promise you, once I get things right, we'll have nothing but time to spend together. Alright?"

Wiping her eyes, Monya gave me a look that clearly spoke of just how disgusted she was, before shaking her head and silently exiting the room.

Watching her walk away, I realized that my household was in a state of disarray. It was also clear to me that unless I tightened up real soon, I would find myself here alone. None of the wealth I had amassed would mean a damn thing to me without my favorite ladies here to share it with me.

Reaching for my Benz keys, I quickly changed my mind and grabbed the keys to the Beamer instead. Instantly warming to the thought that no one else in the city owned the 840, I knew that the sleek luxury of the sports car would more than blow Monique's mind. Yet, what I was even more sure of, was that if the Beamer didn't handle the task, my good loving would finish the job.

With a smirk pasted on my features and my mind racing on thoughts of the night that lay ahead, I placed my household issues on the back burner and exited the safety of my home.

Although I was quick to use the excuse of business to escape captivity, like all other animals who loved the wild and refused to have it any other way, I couldn't wait to reach the jungle.

Chapter 12

"Hey, you two over there! Freeze!" Satin loudly commanded with a menacing scowl. "Don't even think about spending that money with anyone else!"

Looking around to check the scene, he began to spit numerous pre-packaged baggies in his palm. Seeing that he had their undivided attention, he went to work. "This shit is the best product you're gonna find around here." Staring at the two white men directly in their eyes, he said, "If you know like I know, you'll treat yourself, not beat yourself. Now, how much are you two planning to spend with us?" Smiling inwardly, Satin watched them like a hawk.

Exchanging nervous glances between them, they whispered in a low tone. Breaking the short conference, the younger of the two who looked like he needed a hit, stuttered, "Is... this... stuff... real, man?"

Butting in, his partner said, "Look, man. This is our last hundred dollars, and we're just trying not to get beat, you know?"

Stumbling backwards, Satin glared in mock astonishment. "Me? Selling dummy coke! Are you motherfuckers crazy? Do I look like a dummy salesman?" Answering before either of them had the chance, he said, "Hell nah, I don't!" Seeing the indecision that was plastered upon their faces, he snapped, "Give me the damn money!"

Reaching towards Satin with a shaky hand clutching a lone Benjamin, the smoker reluctantly relinquished the money to Satin's forceful grasp. Receiving ten rocks for the money, he called out in alarm to Satin, who had already began to walk away. "Hey, guy! I thought I got twelve for a hundred!"

Frowning, Satin coldly stated, "Hell nah, nigga! Don't even think about twelve of these. As good as this shit is, my own mama couldn't get an extra."

Turning his back on the baffled whites, he grinned at his cunning manner of handling suckers. It was downright hilarious to him that he wouldn't even throw in two extra dummies for a hundred dollars. Heading through the dark alley, he mumbled to himself, "You're one hustling motherfucker, boy!" He was telling the truth, because no one did it like Satin.

Furious, Mann paced back and forth through the plush living room with a black, four-fifth dangling from his hand. Unable to calm him, Supreme, Dax, Ice and Ed watched him in silence as he loudly ranted, "I'm killing his ass on sight!"

"Man, chill!" Supreme snapped, finally tired of his cousin's tirade. "Just kill the nigga when you see him," he stated, using a little reverse psychology. "But just remember that it's a much bigger picture here, so there's a way to do the shit. He's eating big in this city, Mann. So, before you take him out, let's make sure that we're in position to take his place."

Scanning the faces of the men in the room, Mann could tell that they were in agreement with Supreme. Wanting to step his hustle game up, he too understood that for the moment, revenge would have to wait. Calming down, he decided that he wouldn't go searching for Chez. However, if by chance their paths crossed, his guns would bust.

My party had already begun. The blunt smoke I slowly inhaled was rapidly filling my lungs with the euphoric feeling that I craved. Exhaling, I allowed a smoke cloud to float from my open mouth as I winked playfully at Toshia and handed the remainder of the blunt to her.

Receiving the blunt and passing me my cell phone, she informed me that Monique was on her way out.

Glancing at my Rolex to gauge the time, I shook my head in acknowledgement of her words. Deciding that I didn't have an abundance of time, I planned to have Monique somewhere naked and climbing the walls in the next few hours.

Seeing Monique exit her apartment, Qwen climbed from the passenger seat into the back with Toshia. Watching her gracefully stroll towards us, I couldn't help appreciating the sight she presented. Sporting a short silk skirt, matching tube top that showcased her belly ring, and a pair of gold sandals, I was sure that her measurements were somewhere in the range of 36-24-44. Licking my lips at the promising picture, it dawned on me that she was just what I needed to complete my day.

Arriving at the car, she immediately greeted everyone as she made herself comfortable in the soft leather seat.

"This car is really beautiful, Chez." Showing her sexy white smile, she fastened her seatbelt and leaned back.

"Thanks, beautiful," was my reply as I openly appraised every inch of her delicious frame. Allowing my gaze to linger on her swollen glossy lips, I couldn't help but to imagine how good it would feel to suck on them. Pulling out of the parking lot, I could already taste them in my mind.

"Excuse me," she said and blushed. "Where are we headed, and why hasn't anyone passed me any of the good weed I smell?"

"Wherever you want to go is where we're headed, ma."

Watching her grab the blunt from Toshia and take a pull, it was clear to me that as long as our final destination found the two of us somewhere cozy, I couldn't care less where we were headed at that moment. Noticing the sly glance she shot me from the corner of her eye, I began to grin. Maybe it was the weed, but at that moment we both began to laugh. It was crazy that suddenly we both seemed to be on the same page, and the hand she casually dropped into my lap was proof that she may be easier than I'd thought.

Sitting in Craig's house, surrounded by the worst elements of the street, Satin had been smoking crack for hours. Everywhere he looked, someone seemed to have their hand out begging, and he was sick of it. Even as high as he was, Satin could only think of one thing as he stood to leave. This will be my last night getting high. Refusing to throw his life away any longer, he made a vow to get some of the vast riches that were flowing steadily in the streets.

Walking outside into the cool dark night, Satin stood on the porch as he attempted to decide where his next destination would be. Figuring that it didn't make sense to go in with a pocketful of fake cocaine, he decided that the block was where he was headed.

While Mann made the decision not to go looking for Chez, at no time had he promised not to search out members of Chez's crew. With the urge to murder someone heavy on his mind, he, Dax, and Ice patiently laid in wait for the victim they knew would soon show his face.

Mann had no doubt that he would easily catch Satin. Unlike the rest of his old crew, Satin was a free spirit who got high and couldn't care less if they liked it or not. Only, Mann knew that if Satin was unlucky enough to have come out tonight, he would leave the world wishing that he had chosen to stay home instead.

Juggling strategies in his mind that would place him back on top, Satin happily strolled through the block. More excited than he had been in months, he realized that blowing up would be easy once he showed his old crew that he had straightened up. A spot had always awaited him, and he was aware that all he needed to do the whole time was reach out and grab it. He was ready now, and even as happy as he was, he could only imagine how happy Chez would be to have him back on track.

Smiling, something told Satin to look up at that moment. Immediately alarmed at the sight of three hooded figures stepping out of the shadows, he felt that something about the trio just didn't seem right. Halting his steps, he instinctively began to search for an escape route, to no avail.

Slowly backpedaling in preparation for an all-out sprint if necessary, he stopped in his tracks at the sight of a big pistol appearing in the hand of the middle figure. Not sure what was happening, he quickly began to think about the different people he had beaten lately.

Enjoying the look of fear on Satin's face, Mann slowly removed the hood that hid his features from Satin. Watching the way his eyes widened at the moment of recognition, Mann hissed, "Say your prayers, nigga!"

At that moment, Satin attempted to run. Releasing a few slugs from the four-fifth, Mann stared through blood red beady eyes as the force of two bullets ripped through Satin's back, throwing him face first in the street.

"Ahhh!" Satin cried out in pain as his face crashed down on the pavement.

Hearing their approaching footsteps and unable to rise, he attempted to crawl away. Wanting to live, he was aware that his chances of escaping from Mann at this point were slim to none. However, he refused to just give up on life without at least trying.

Watching him crawl, Mann took quick, smooth steps that were more than enough to catch up with the injured Satin. Reaching him, he placed a large Timberland on the back of his neck and commanded in a flat, heartless tone, "Finish him off, Dax."

With no words said, Dax stepped up and removed a chrome pistol grip .357 Magnum from his waist.

"No-o-o-o!" Satin screamed. Babbling in an attempt to save his life, he pleaded, "Don't do this, man! What have I done?"

Pointing the revolver at Satin's head, Dax squeezed off three shots. Without blinking, he watched as the first tore a huge chunk out of the left side of Satin's head. The two that followed only met the red gore that was the remains of brain tissue and fragments of skull. Observing his work with no emotion, Dax placed the revolver back in his waistband and walked away without another glance at the body.

Grinning slyly, Mann thought to himself that the death of Satin was the beginning of their takeover. Proud of their work, he walked off with Ice by his side.

Hearing the sounds of gunshots close by, Gator hesitantly rose up from the position he had been nodding in. Nosily peering through the filthy cracked windows of the abandoned house, he witnessed Mann, Ice and Dax quickly moving through the cut. Thinking that someone had to be dead for the three of them to be lurking in the darkness, he scratched his groin and sat back down on the dirty mattress.

Immediately returning to his previous state, the feel of the good dope removed any other thoughts that he may have had.

Pulling away from Qwen's truck, I popped in a slow tape. Letting Keith Sweat work his magic, I too planned to be working mine real soon.

Noticing the way Monique was reclined in the passenger seat with her eyes closed as she grooved to the smooth sounds pouring out of the Bose system, I thought, Yeah, Keith! The sudden sight of her skirt sitting high on the tops of her smooth, thick red thighs made my blood boil. She had had the same effect on me throughout the night, what I now stared at with lust filled eyes had me hard as steel.

Opening her eyes and catching me in the process, Monique gave me one of the cutest dimpled smiles. Running her moist, pink tongue subtly over her succulent lips, she jokingly questioned, "Do you like what you see?"

Nodding my head in the affirmative, I was sure that my smile made it more than clear that I liked what I saw a whole lot. Changing the subject, I asked, "Did you enjoy yourself, ma?"

Leaning towards me, she whispered, "So far I have enjoyed myself a lot. I'm only hoping that the night isn't over yet."

Finishing her statement, she leaned all the way in and placed her lips against mine. Enjoying the way she worked her tongue, I loved the minty wet taste of her mouth. Just from the kiss alone, it was entirely too apparent that other hidden talents would soon be revealed.

Breaking our kiss, she stared at me with glazed over eyes as she rubbed my head affectionately. "Chez, you need to hurry up and get to my house," she informed in a hoarse voice.

Pushing down harder on the accelerator, the BMW shot forward, throwing her back in the seat. I was ready to get her home, and the sight of her lavender panties peeking from beneath her raised skirt gave me the indication that I would arrive at exactly where I wanted to be.

Giving Ice and Dax pounds, Mann roared, "One down, fellows! Now we've got five more to go!"

Laughing, Ice agreed. "We definitely got one of them. I never liked his punk ass anyway. We should have killed him the last time we shot his crack smoking ass." Sucking his teeth, he asked, "When do we get the rest of them, dog?"

"Real soon," Man replied, smiling wickedly. "We will definitely catch them out there before it's over with. And when we do, they won't see it coming."

Saying nothing, Dax continued smoking his Newport. In his mind, he was rationalizing the bullshit Mann had just told Ice. No one could help but figure out what had taken place tonight. First, Chez knocked Mann out, then Satin turns up dead. How coincidental could two such events be?

Tossing the cigarette in the ashtray, Dax was aware that after tonight, there would be no more surprises, regardless of what Mann said. Nevertheless, whether they had the element of surprise at their disposal or not, he couldn't care less. When it came down to it, Dax was prepared for the drama however it came.

We were barely inside the apartment before we were all over one another. Kissing and groping like two teens, her sandals were the only article of clothing she still wore. Discarding clothing as fast as we possibly could, her dress, bra, tank top and panties were scattered amongst my clothing on the living room floor.

With only my socks and jewelry on, I held Monique up against the wall with her legs wrapped around my waist. Listening to her rapid breaths, I took turns ravaging her soft juicy lips, and a pair of the thickest brown nipples I had ever had the pleasure of sucking on in my life.

"That feels so good, Chez!" Gently raking her nails down my spine, she whimpered, "Keep sucking them just like that, boo!"

Hearing her words, I was too far-gone to answer. Instead, I gripped two palms full of her soft red ass cheeks and spread them apart. Inserting my middle finger between her folds, I received a shock at how wet and tight I found her to be.

Moaning excitedly as I probed her insides, she placed her palms on either side of my face, stared deep into my eyes and kissed me long and hard. Reaching between us, she wrapped her hand around my shaft and placed it at her opening. Giving me a sincere, pleading look, she whispered, "It's been a long time, Chez. Please, be gentle with me."

Unable to contain myself any longer, I pulled her hips downward, and thrust upwards into her glove-tight warmth.

"Oooh, God!" she wailed loudly at the force of my invasion. Sucking in a breath as if she were drowning, she sank her teeth into my shoulder as I continued deep stroking her.

Feeling myself about to reach the first climax, I increased the intensity of my strokes as she raked her nails over my back and hollered like I was killing her.

"Chez! Chez! Oh shit, Chez! I've waited so long for this, baby!"

Feeling the first spurt erupt into her, my trembling legs gave out, causing us to fall on the thick, plush carpeting. No sooner than we landed, I felt our roles reverse. Suddenly, she was on top, and instead of it being me who pounded her, it was Monique who vigorously rode me.

Moaning lightly as I felt my toes curling up, I heard her say to the clapping sound of her ass slamming down upon my stomach, "This pussy belongs to you, baby!"

Loving the way her shit was feeling, I glanced down at my Rolex. After seeing the time, I realized that late or not, my work was cut out for me. Slowly beginning to thrust upwards, I figured I might as well give her a reason to make all the noise she was already making.

Chapter 13

It seemed as if I never had a free moment for myself. Between setting aside time to deal with Monya, Neeta and Monique, plus running back and forth to New York on a constant basis, my schedule was swamped.

My hands had already been full before, but suddenly everyone in the city, as well as those that bordered my own, were buying their weight from me and my crew. Selling over forty keys weekly, the money I was seeing was nothing short of astronomical. However, with the exception of Qwen and Bocca who supplied me, no one else really had the slightest idea of just how major I had become.

Hearing my phone, I hit the remote, turning the blaring system down a few decibels. "Yeah, what's up?" I spoke into the receiver.

"Hey, Daddy!" Neeta excitedly responded. "Where are you, Chez?"

"Hey, baby. I'm not too far from you. Why?"

Babbling as usual, she said, "I need some money, baby. I saw the most beautiful bedroom set earlier, and I just have to own it. You said I can furnish the house however I wanted to, so can I get it?"

"How much do you need, Neeta?" I had already set aside a large sum for her to use however she saw fit when I told her that she could get the house and car done in the manner of her choosing. Therefore, the question was merely for my amusement.

"Oh, baby, you're gonna love it! They're asking five grand for it, but I'll need about another two grand for sheets, comforters and drapes. I can't wait 'til you're able to see it, baby. It's huge, and it has netting that cascades to the floor on all sides. And guess what, Chez?"

Figuring that I had better cut her short, I said, "Listen, Neeta. I have to handle some business, then I'll swing by there and drop the money off. I gotta go, baby."

"Alright then," she said with a level of sulking evident in her tone. "Hurry up though. I need to get it as soon as I possibly can. Plus, I'm horny, so I need to get that taken care of as soon as possible too, okay?"

Chuckling, I said, "I won't be long, baby. I gotta go, Neeta, so just hold tight and all your problems will get taken care of."

Shaking my head, I ended our call with the thought that too many people looked to me for their survival. And even though it wasn't a problem, I realized that in order for me to continue holding them down, I couldn't slip in my own game. In my mind, I refused to let them down.

Drifting off in thought, I found myself wondering whether I had let Satin down. Could I have possibly saved him? If not, why did his death weigh so heavily on my conscience after all these months? Recalling the fateful day over a year ago when our relationship came apart, I drove in a daze…

A Year Earlier

Things had just begun to take a turn for the better. In acquiring my first brick, I had moved into a much more elevated stage of the game. With a new car and more luxurious living arrangements, it was clear that '92 would be my year for change.

Since returning home over six months earlier, I had made a major leap from where I'd been, to the point I now found myself at as I cruised through the strip, searching for Satin. For some reason, he had been missing in action, and I was on a mission to find him. Pulling up to the curb at a gathering of young thugs, I rolled down the window and asked, "Have any of you seen Satin?"

With the exception of Little Cook, all the other homies shook their heads and nervously turned away. Giving them mean mugs, Cook stepped over to the car. "Yo, Chez, that nigga's held up in Craig's spot." Lowering his tone, he spoke in a conspiratorial manner, "I don't know what's up, man, but he's been there ever since yesterday." Giving me a pound, he turned to walk away, but not before tossing the words over his shoulder, "You didn't hear it from me."

Catching his meaning immediately, I was instantly pissed off as I pulled away from the curb, heading in the direction of Craig's house. There was no logical reason why Satin would be held up in a crack house for 24 hours, unless he had gone back on his word and returned to his previous addiction.

Arriving at the house, I bailed out of the car. Walking straight into Craig's house, I began my search for Satin.

Rising up from his seat on an old, tattered couch, Craig attempted to swell his skinny chest as he snapped, "Yo, Chez! What the hell you think you're doing rolling up in my shit like you own it?" Stepping in my way, he glared through evil little slits as if I was supposed to have been deterred.

Shooting out a short right jab that connected with his glass jaw, I sent him reeling to the filthy, burnt carpet. Watching the remainder of smokers around me scatter out of the way, I stepped over his still form and continued my search.

Opening every door as I stormed through the house, I was caught off guard when I pushed the last door open at the end of the hall, and came face to face with my partner sitting up in bed naked, with the stem in his mouth and a skinny smoker sucking him off.

Noticing me standing in the doorway, Satin removed the stem, blew out a cloud of smoke and nonchalantly spoke in a foggy voice, "What's going on, bro?"

Looking up with a blank stare, the skinny smoker cleared her throat. Then, as if it were a normal occurrence, she went back to the task of forcing as much of Satin back down her throat as possible.

At a loss for words, I couldn't believe that this was Satin. Between the disgust and disappointment I was feeling, the only thing I could do was stand there with my mouth agape as I scanned the perimeter of the room. Seeing a clear sandwich bag on the nightstand that seemed to hold around three ounces, I asked, "What the fuck are you doing, man?"

Taking another hit from the pipe, Satin closed his eyes for a brief moment before gently lifting his bottom lip and coolly stating, "I'm doing me, Chez. Damn!"

"Oh yeah? You're doing you, huh?" I questioned, wanting to check his chin too.

"Yeah, nigga! You heard me!" he snapped. "This is how I'm carrying it. My money's long, and regardless of whether you or anyone else likes it, this is how it's gonna be."

"Okay, Satin. If that's how you feel, then the decision has already been made." Speaking slowly and in as precise a manner as I possibly could, I said, "I hope that you are prepared to live with your decision man, because any dealings we once had are over." Meaning what I was about to say from the bottom of my heart, I looked him directly in the eye and added, "As of this moment, you're on your own."

Raising the pipe back towards his mouth, he gave me a look of revulsion before laughing in my face, followed by a defiant command to close the door on my way out.

Glancing back one last time as I exited the room, it saddened me to see Satin with the stem hanging from the corner of his mouth, with his eyes closed and a hand tangled in the short, nappy hair of the smoker...

Snapping out of my dream state, I spotted my man's BMW up ahead. The three keys I carried for him was proof of how far I had come. But if I ever found out who had murdered Satin, I wouldn't hesitate to set everything I'd acquired to the side and go back to the old Chez.

Pulling to a stop beside my dog's whip, I reached for the bag containing the bricks. As I hit the handle to open the door, it dawned on me that sooner or later, it would come to light who was responsible. When that time arrived, they would pay with their lives.

Parading through her large Colonial style house, Neeta was in diva mode. The silk and chiffon nightie she wore barely covered any of her womanly parts, but that was exactly how she wanted it. Figuring that it wouldn't hurt to have Chez lusting over her, she had taken a soothing aromatherapy bath in her newly installed tub. Afterwards, she had taken her time rubbing vanilla scented Victoria's Secret lotion over every inch of her body. Looking and smelling good, she had no doubt that before the end of the day, she would have Chez eating out of her palm, and a few other places, as usual.

Laughing at the thought of some of the freaky shit he had done to her, Neeta had to admit that he had a major up on all the rest when it came to the bedroom. However, like every other male she had set out to snag, he too had fallen for her game; hook, line and sinker.

"Poor fools!" she spoke out loud as she sipped her early evening concoction of champagne and orange juice. "Umph, umph, umph!" she muttered, using her tongue to catch a drop that was trying to escape down her chin.

Plopping down in the plush sitting room chair, Neeta took in the scene of pure luxury around her. This is the life! she grinned in thought. Yet, what was even more exciting, was that this time around, the house, car, jewels and everything else she had received from Chez were truly hers.

Deciding that this was only the beginning, she rationalized that although she would never allow herself to love Chez, she could surely put up with him if he continued to take care of her in such a royal manner as this. The only question was, what was she going to do about poor, in love Monya? In order to accomplish her goal of being Chez's one and only, she would have to devise a plan to get rid of his wifey.

Sucking on her manicured index finger, Neeta contemplated her next course of action. If all else fell into place, the problem Monya presented would be taken care of on its own.

Not trying to hear the bullshit coming through the receiver, Supreme snapped, "Look, nigga! No more excuses, and I mean it! You have 24 hours to come up with my loot. And if you're not ringing this phone with a time and place for us to meet, your country ass is dead! Now, do I make myself clear?"

"Yeah, man. You're clear," Butter replied. But, I—"

"But, my ass!" Supreme growled, and hung up the phone.

Glaring angrily, he shook his head at the realization that Butter was as good as dead if he didn't come up with his thirty-five grand. Unable to understand the mentality of down South niggas, he decided that even with the losses, Virginia was a gold mine. The only problem was, if he wasn't careful, they would have to murder everyone in the city before they obtained the riches for themselves.

Jerking his head around to see if his eyes had played tricks on him, Supreme slowed the Maxima to a creep. Grinning, he found that his eyes hadn't tricked him after all. In his view was the red Lexus, and beautiful driver that he had spent the last few months in search of.

Thinking that today had to be his lucky day, he whipped a U-turn while exclaiming, "I've got your pretty ass now, ma!"

Talking to the happily squealing baby as she tucked her into her car seat, Monya caught a sideways glimpse of a burgundy Maxima heading towards them. Halting her one sided conversation with Chanae, she narrowed her eyes in an attempt to see the driver's identity through the tinted windows. Unable to do so, she raised from her crouched position and closed the car door. On guard, she stared with alert eyes as the Maxima pulled to a stop beside her and slowly rolled down the driver's window.

Catching her breath, for some unknown reason the smile that appeared on her face at the moment her heartbeat increased was unlike anything she had ever experienced. Unable to speak, she stood rooted to the spot as she locked eyes with the handsome New Yorker who had been on her mind for the last few months.

Maintaining eye contact, Supreme was mesmerized by the flawless beauty that stood before him. Willing to wager that no other in the city could compare to his mystery woman, he concluded that after the high and low search he had been through in order to find her, he wasn't about to let her get away. Breaking the silence, he gave her his most sincere dimpled smile. "So, we meet again, huh?"

Shifting uncomfortably from foot to foot, Monya returned his smile and replied, "I guess it does look that way." Only, in her head, the words "finally" and "about time" were screaming to get out.

Openly gawking at her, Supreme announced, "Please don't take this the wrong way, but you're so beautiful!" Shaking his head in disbelief, he chewed his bottom lip in awe before continuing. "Ever since our near collision, you're all I've been able to think of. I have actually searched every inch of this city for you. Now that I've found you, I need your help in insuring that I'm not going to lose you again."

Wringing her hands nervously, Monya was flattered by his revelation. Blushing, she said, "That was really sweet. But in all honesty, it sounds like some real good game." Grinning at his raised eyebrow due to her declaration, she decided to play along by asking a question of her own. "For the hell of it, let's just say that I did believe you. Why should I help you not to lose me?" Awaiting his reply with a rapidly beating heart, she hoped that his answer would be worthy of the risk they were taking by playing such a dangerous game.

Staring into his sincere eyes, she wondered if he had any idea who she really was. And if he did, could he have had the slightest idea of how quickly Chez would murder him.

Locked in a staring match with Monya, Supreme responded with confidence, "That's easy. You should help me because not only do I want you, I need you. Therefore, we're in search of the same things, being that you need to be wanted, and want to be needed." Gauging her response to his words by the rapid rise and fall of her chest and unblinking stare, he continued. "My guess is that you're taken, but I can't help wondering whether you're being taken care of in the manner that I would undoubtedly take care of you." Reaching out a hand that held a card, he said, "If ever you need to be treated like the queen that you are, give me a call, beautiful." Licking his lips in a promising manner, he broke their stare and slowly pulled off.

Watching him leave after appearing out of thin air and giving her all the right reasons to take a risk and holler at him, Monya stood in open mouthed amazement. Tired of putting her life on hold while Chez lived it up, she decided that she would definitely give him a call. It's time that I experience some excitement of my own, she thought, placing the card in the pocket of her shearling coat. Surprised by the tingling sensation she had experienced due to his words alone, the mere thought of what his touch would be like made her moisten.

Getting in the car, Monya's mind was made up. If Chez could do it, so could she. Now, it only boiled down to how she could go about it without getting caught.

Wondering to himself if she would get in contact with him, Supreme's gut feeling told him that she would. Feeling that he had played his hand appropriately, he concluded that if and when she did call, he would pull out all the necessary stops to blow her mind.

Even with the plans he had for Chez that would turn his silver-spooned life into a living hell, he truly wanted Monya. With the vast number of women who fought for his attention, he couldn't quite figure out what made her stand so far in front of the crowd. She was just different, and that was all there was to it. Besides the fact that Chez wouldn't have any use for her where he was headed, Supreme had already made up his mind that she would be his woman when all was said and done.

Figuring that he had been patient long enough, Supreme decided that the time had arrived to set his plans in motion.

Calculating the flow of constant business transactions I had encountered throughout the day, I had stacked over eighty grand, and I was only too aware that each member of my crew had either matched that number or surpassed it. Therefore, I had no choice but to admit that today had been a great day.

Speaking of great, even now as I whipped through the I-95 traffic at maximum speed, I couldn't erase the thoughts of my highly enjoyable, lengthy session of lovemaking with Neeta. She was without a doubt worth, the seven grand she had cost me today, not to mention the other vast amounts of money I'd dropped on her up to this point. To be completely honest, if it weren't for Monya and the fact that the title of wifey belonged exclusively to her, Neeta would hold it hands down.

Speeding up the off ramp, I rolled to a stop at the tollbooth that would allow me access into the city. Reaching out of the window to drop a quarter into the slot, I felt my phone begin to vibrate. Snatching it off my hip at the same moment I raced through the blockade, I spoke into the receiver. "Yeah, what's up?"

"You're the one who controls the world, compadre. So, why don't you give me the answer to that question?" the caller replied slyly.

Immediately recognizing the voice, I smiled. "No, my friend. It is you who made it possible for this little portion of the world to fall under my control. Therefore, as always, you have all the answers."

Laughing heartily, Bocca stated, "You are too wise, Chez. And I'm lucky to have you in my family. Now, my reason for calling, I'm having a party tomorrow night and I would really appreciate it if you and your people would make an appearance. If this notice is too late, I will understand if you're unable to make it."

"Unable to make it! Psst! Imagine that! We'll be there. Just don't expect us until after midnight. And, I want you to know that I only put my operation on pause for you, Bocca. No one else."

"For that, my friend, I am grateful. I must go and deal with other pressing issues, but I expect to receive your call as soon as you reach New York. Okay?"

"Cool. I'm out," I stated, ending our call.

Replacing the phone, I began to make a mental checklist of necessities. The first thing that needed to be done was to have someone make reservations on American Airlines for my whole crew to fly first class. Secondly, they would need to reserve a whip that was worthy of our star status. It needed to be ready as soon as we landed. Snubbing my nose at the mere thought of having to arrive at the party in a cab, looking like millionaires, made me pick my phone back up and dial 411.

Listening to the phone ringing, I figured that I would handle all the reservations myself, then put together an outfit to rival all others. This would in no way be a regular party. The guests that would be gathered for this event would no doubt give the word "baller" a new meaning. With that thought in mind, I too planned to show that my crew and I were far from average.

Chapter 14

Being back in New York felt good. This was exactly what I needed, because my hectic business schedule could stand to be set aside, if only for a few days. Leaning further back into the soft, comfortable leather seat, I inwardly grinned at the thought that having all this money wouldn't make a bit of sense if I never took the time to spend it like the baller that I was.

"Yo, this joint rides smooth," Dresser commented, punching his foot down on the accelerator and glancing at Sam in the passenger seat. "Remind me to add one of these to my fleet when we get home," Dresser boasted with a wink.

"Check this nigga out!" I stated, leaning towards Qwen. "Suddenly, he's the ultimate baller, huh?" Chuckling, I repeated his words, "Remind me to add one of these to my fleet when we get home!"

Smiling, Qwen reached over the seat and tapped Dresser playfully upside his head. "Oh, you don't have to count on Sam to remind your big spending ass. I'll be more than happy to do it for him. That way, I can just borrow your shit instead of buying my own."

Dipping in and out of traffic, Dresser snapped, "You better buy your own, nigga! Because when I cop me a Jaguar, I'll be the only one pushing that shit."

Reaching for the blunt Sam was extending between the seats, I said, "Slow this bitch down, nigga, before you fuck around and tear it up. I'd hate for your ass to be buying this one before we even make it back home," I taunted, taking a toke of the good green.

"Chill, Chez! Damn! I got this!" he frowned before adding, "If I do crash this bitch, it ain't like I can't buy it."

Laughing along with the others at Dresser's proclamation, I had no doubt that his paper allowed him to easily purchase another whip if necessary. My only argument to the contrary was I wasn't trying to get killed in this one in order to prove it.

Pointing up ahead, Sam said, "Damn! Look at all the people and traffic packed in front of that club, fellows!"

Snapping out of my previous thoughts, I saw that he was right. The assembled crowd was ridiculous. The line stretched around the back, and luxury vehicles were double-parked as far as the eye could see. Cruising into the sea of Benz's, Limousines, Range Rovers and Beamers, I heard Qwen excitedly state, "This shit is gonna be off the hook!"

Turning to face him, I smiled at the sight of him busily rechecking his appearance. Shaking my head, I teased, "Nigga, you look just fine."

In all honesty, we all looked good, and I had no doubt that we would make great impressions on everyone who counted.

Reaching for my phone to alert Bocca of our arrival, I instructed Dresser, "Pull right in front of the door, player." Planning on making a grand entrance, I realized that the only way to accomplish that was to have the crowd witness us exiting the Jaguar directly in front of the door. "Yeah, Bocca, we're here," I informed him.

"Where are you located, mi compadre?"

"Dresser just pulled up in front of the door, man."

Alright, Chez. I'll have someone come take care of your car, and lead you all to me." Bocca stated, ending the call.

Shutting the phone off, I glanced around the whip at the questioning faces of my crew. "What?" I grinned. "You niggas already know we're the stars, so it shouldn't be too surprising that someone is on the way to park our shit and lead us straight through the ropes." Seeing the grins that immediately appeared on their faces, I seriously added. "When it comes to us, there will never be anything short of VIP from this point on."

Realizing that she hadn't driven the Q45 in ages, Monya decided that since she wasn't trying to draw any unnecessary attention, it wouldn't be smart for her to take the Lexus, Beamer or Benz out tonight. The last thing she wanted was to be noticed while carrying out the mission she had planned for the night.

Deciding that Chez couldn't have picked a better time to leave town, she concluded that it was the perfect time to use the card Supreme gave her had been burning her pocket terribly. In a state of disarray, she nervously reached for the phone on numerous occasions, only to change her mind in the end. However, after going over all of the indiscretions she was aware of Chez carelessly committing, she had finally gathered the courage to make the call. That had taken place hours prior to the thoughts she now experienced as she sped down the highway in route to their pre-arranged rendezvous spot.

Still somewhat nervous, Monya couldn't help snickering at the thoughts that ran through her mind. Thinking that she was after nothing more than a good orgasm, she wondered what could have possibly gotten into her to have her acting so recklessly. Mumbling the words, "Nothing has gotten into me," she saw the sign overhead that notified her that she was nearing her exit. Sighing, she stated, "I sure hope that your sexy ass knows how to fuck, Supreme. If I lose Chez behind this shit, I at least want tonight to be worth it!"

Refusing to be late for his rendezvous with Monya, Supreme checked his watch to make sure that he was still on schedule. After all the months he had dreamed of getting with her, the last thing he planned to do was give her a bad impression.

Grabbing his phone, he began dialing Mann's number, while reaching to lower the music with his free hand. Hearing the voice on the other end, he got straight to the point. "Yo, it's me, Supreme. I need you to do me a favor, cuz. Swing past Zo's house. He has some dough for me, alright?"

"It's not a problem, man. But how much money am I supposed to be getting from him?" Mann questioned.

"He's holding twenty gees, cuz. Damn! It almost slipped my mind. Take care of Lil' Qwen while you're at it, cuz. He wants two keys, and he'll be waiting over Zo's spot too."

Frowning at the phone he held, Mann said, "Yeah, I'll handle it, Preme. Now, how about you tell me what you're doing that's so important that you can't find time to pick up over sixty-five grand? That's not like you, fam."

Seeing the exit up ahead, Supreme blurted, "I can't explain right now, but I will say that what I'm doing fits in with all our plans. Look, just handle that for me, and trust me, alright?"

"Alright, cuz. Just handle your business then. I'm out."

Replacing his phone, Supreme hit the exit ramp that he hoped would not only take him to the restaurant they had arranged to meet at, but to the adjoining hotel before the end of the night.

Grinning at the thought of actually sleeping with Monya, it suddenly dawned on him that inside his pocket, he held a natural concoction called "stone". It was proven many times over to make any woman who he used it on lose her mind. It had never let him down. If she allowed him to work his magic, tonight would be no different.

With nothing but thoughts of punishing Monya in mind, Supreme concluded that the good loving he would give her would only ruin her for any other man who came along afterwards.

Smiling, he stated, "I just hope your pussy can compete with the rest of you that seems so perfect, Monya. If so, I promise that you will be my woman before it's over with."

Pulling up to the restaurant, he said, "Let the games begin."

Leaning against his new Acura, Boo-Boo watched the traffic that flowed non-stop through the block. Volunteering to remain behind while the rest of the crew went to Bocca's party, he used the excuse that someone needed to watch over their vast operation. Yet, his real reason for wanting to remain behind was that he loved the block. Fuck a damn New York! was what he really thought. Instead of trying to showboat for a bunch of fake, frontin' ass niggas who he hated anyway, he found solace right where he stood, in the center of Mistletoe and Harding Streets.

"Yo, Boo-Boo! What's up, you fly, ballin' ass motherfucker?"

Turning towards the approaching voice, Boo-Boo's face lit up with an instant grin. Although grinning was something that he rarely did, the sight of Gator pimping hard on some '70's shit, and the dopefiend lingo he knew would soon be flowing from his mouth, was more than enough to make him soften. Even though Boo-Boo would never give him the benefit of hearing it from his mouth, he actually liked the old school player.

Receiving the pound Gator shot out, Boo-Boo said, "I'm just lounging, trying to keep an eye on my money, pimp. What's with you though?"

Speaking through barely opened lips while scratching at his scraggly bearded chin, he drawled, "You know me, baby. Ol' Gator's out here on the grind, while trying to duck the time." Letting his words sink in as he appraised Boo-Boo's new ride, he shook his head up and down in appreciation. "Yeah, your shit is as official as a referee with a whistle, young nigga." Placing the most serious look he could muster upon his face, he stared at Boo-Boo with his hands out and palms up. "Uh… what's the chances of Ol' Gator hitting on you for a few dollars, fly guy?"

Laughing inside at the pure con that had just been tried on him, Boo-Boo kept a straight, emotionless face as he replied, "Old school, you already know I ain't coming up off no dough. I'm out here trying to stack a fortune, pimp. If I give my shit to you, I may as well give every motherfucker around here free reign to go in my pockets."

Contemplating Boo-Boo's answer, he shook his head before agreeing. "You know what? You're right, fly guy. Ol' Gator sees your point." Glancing around them suspiciously, he lowered his tone and said, "Let's just say that I had a little information to trade for the help you really want to throw me anyway. Then what?"

"Yeah, whatever, nigga!" Boo-Boo responded, uninterested.

Deciding that he had more important things to do, and Gator couldn't possibly have any information that he would want, he concluded that Gator had all but worn out his welcome.

"Hey, Boo!" the packed car of cuties called out simultaneously as they passed.

Nonchalantly throwing up his hand in reply, Boo-Boo glanced at Gator and sucked his teeth in irritation. "Okay, humor me, old school. What you got for me, man?"

Catching him by surprise, Gator asked, "Did your crew ever find out who killed Satin, fly guy?"

Removing a forty-five from the small of his back and placing it on the car, Boo-Boo glared evilly and snapped, "Tell me what you know, and don't play any games either, Gator!"

Having already weighed his options before deciding to tell the young live-wire what he had witnessed, Gator sighed as he warily eyed the pistol.

"The night Satin was murdered, I was in the abandoned house around the corner, nodding off on some of that good tar." Shaking his head as if the memory had been a special one, he slowly continued. "Anyway, as I was nodding, I heard gunshots. When I raised up and took a look to see what was going on, I saw those 5th Ward niggas, Mann, Dax and Ice, hurrying through the cut with hoods on."

In a rapidly increasing rage, Boo-Boo spoke through clenched teeth. "Who else have you told this to, Gator?"

Nervously glancing from Boo-Boo to the four-fifth he held tightly in his grasp, Gator blurted, "You're the only one I've told, fly guy. No one else knows I saw anything."

Reaching inside his pocket, Boo-Boo extracted a large knot of bills and tossed them to Gator. Hurrying towards the driver's side of the Acura, he made his meaning as clear as it could possibly be when he raised the four-fifth to point in Gator's face. "We never had this conversation," Boo-Boo growled. "You hear me?"

Rapidly nodding his head yes, Gator stared at Boo-Boo through unblinking eyes with a mixture of excitement and fear plastered on his face. As if he had moved with lightning speed, he watched the young gangster peel off up the block with tires spinning.

Suddenly alarmed that he was standing in the middle of one of the most dangerous blocks in the city, Gator hurriedly tucked the knot of bills in his pocket. Knowing how hungry niggas in the street were, and being known to slice a throat himself in his own times of greed, he suspiciously stared around him as he did a rapid calculation of what he thought the knot contained after one quick thumb-through. Having too much money himself at one point, he was a wizard at speed counting and eyeballing bankrolls. That was why he now moved quickly down the street with the biggest toothless smile to grace his features in years. If his numbers were correct, and all the bills he held in his pocket were Benjamins, today was truly his lucky day. How long that luck would last was questionable, but for the moment, Gator was ten grand ahead of the game.

Popping the stash spot as he sped through the block, Boo-Boo removed the twin to the four-fifth he held on his lap. Heading home to change, he planned to set a mission in motion that wouldn't end until much blood had been shed. Realizing that he would have to do it alone since his crew was out of town, and he trusted no one else enough to take them along, he prepared himself for the solo war that was inevitable.

Furious, he mumbled, "You niggas want drama, and on the blood of my family, I promise to give you all you want and more!"

Whipping through traffic, Boo-Boo was prepared to kill or be killed.

The party that was laid out before us was proof that Bocca had outdone himself. Already used to the finer things that came along with having money, even I found myself in awe at the sight of the unexpected scene we stepped into.

New York's elite had come out en masse to celebrate with Bocca, and the extravagant riches that they carelessly donned were unbelievable. With that thought in mind, my ego was automatically swollen, because for us to be in attendance alone, spoke of just how far we had come up through the ranks in a relatively short period of time.

Grabbing glasses of champagne from a tray that was carried by one of the many meagerly dressed dimepieces that were serving, we made our way through the tightly packed club. The attention we blatantly drew from the wall to wall beauties that we passed on our way to the VIP room made it clear that we not only held our own, we stood out.

Draped in a three-quarter length mink, teal wool slacks, a dark green, thin silk button down shirt, and black gators to match, I knew that I was a sight for sore eyes. The diamond studded Jesus piece that hung from the big Gucci link that sat on my neck, along with the Presidential Rolex and diamond studded bracelet set the outfit off perfectly.

Raising the crystal glass to my lips, my eyes caught the reflection of the diamond sparkling on my pinky finger at the same moment that I noticed a small group of gold diggers staring with their mouths agape. Loving the attention, I winked in their direction and took a sip from the glass while continuing on my path towards the VIP section, thinking that our crew was major.

Arriving at the roped off VIP area, Bocca appeared from out of what seemed like thin air. Halting the security guards who were in the process of frisking us, he sternly stated, "They don't have to be subjected to that, fellows." Giving me a hug, he said, "They're my special guests," before ushering us through the rope. "Come, my friends," he informed, leading us towards a large circular table full of beautiful Puerto Rican women.

Leaning in close to my ear, Bocca whispered, "If you or your people see anything..." grinning slyly he stressed, "...And I do mean anything at all that you want, let me know, alright, my friend?"

Although I was more than sure that whatever we may have wanted we could have, I respectfully replied, "You will undoubtedly be the first to know if that's the case, Bocca."

Reaching the table first, I glimpsed the seat I wanted quickly, and staked an unspoken claim on the dime-piece who sat next to me with a sly, fleeting glance as I coolly continued my conversation with Bocca.

Taking our seats, we were quickly introduced to the women, who turned out to be our special guests for the night. Peering around the table at some of the beauties that my crew had positioned themselves next to, I made a mental note to remember to give Bocca his props on the rare choices he had made where the ladies were concerned.

"Well, Chez, you and your people feel free to order anything you may want or need. I have to leave for a moment to mingle with some of my other guests." Patting me on the shoulder, he turned to stare at each of the ladies. "I want you each to treat my friends as if they were royalty. Have I made myself clear?" he sternly questioned.

Receiving a nod of understanding from each of them, Bocca winked at me and proceeded to move off in the direction of another group of guests.

"Hi. I'm Aneesa," my special hostess stated, moving in closer. "From the moment I saw you heading in this direction, I had already picked you as the one I wanted to meet." Smiling seductively, she bit down sexily on her bottom lip and said, "I'm glad you also decided that your best choice was right here beside me too, Chez."

Although beautiful women had always been a luxury that I was afforded regularly, Aneesa wasn't the usual beauty by any means. Sporting the body of a highly sought after stripper, a deliciously thick set of cherry red full lips, and the longest wavy hair I had ever laid eyes on, she easily made the baddest bitch bow out. However, it was the gray eyes that held the promise of hidden pleasures behind them that made her a flawless beauty in my eyes. Taking a sip of my champagne, I grinned slyly at the realization that before the night was over, I would be tapping into the array of pleasures that I'm sure she possessed.

Taking notice of the conversation and smiles around me, it was apparent that like myself, my crew and their new acquaintances were forming relationships that would lead to their receiving pleasures as well before the night's end.

Suddenly thinking about the women I had left at home, I found myself wondering if they would carry it as messed up as me if they had the chance. With Monique, I had no doubt in my mind that she would. I was hitting it at every available moment, while her man was in jail without bond. I couldn't really be sure with Neeta, because although I couldn't catch her in any type of compromising positions, I realized that she was slick. However, I knew that Monya would always remain pure and trustworthy. Regardless of the questions I had pertaining to the others, I never had to worry about my boo, Monya.

Feeling Aneesa's hand roaming up my thigh, quickly erased any other thoughts I may have had about Monya, Neeta or Monique. Reaching beneath the table to begin my exploration up her thick, walnut-complexioned thighs, I concluded that tonight I belonged to the Puerto Rican goddess beside me. Finding no barrier as my fingers slid between her pre-soaked lips, I could honestly say that at that moment, what we were about to embark upon was all that mattered.

Chapter 15

Wondering what the hell she had gotten herself into, Monya loudly gasped in an attempt to catch her breath, feeling as if she would faint at any moment due to the vicious assault that Supreme was putting her through. "Umm! Supreme! Supreme! Oh God, Supreme!" she whimpered as she grasped the sheets to support herself against the force of his pounding.

Besides the loud clapping sounds of flesh pounding against flesh, her excited moans and the little animalistic cries that poured from her mouth only added to Supreme's excitement. Grinning while rapidly rotating his hips in a grinding motion, he purposely forced himself deeper inside her, enjoying the frenzied state he had her in.

"Oooh! Oooh! Oooh!" Monya cried into the pillow.

Feeling him deep inside her stomach, her legs trembled uncontrollably as she fought to stay on her hands and knees. After two hours of non-stop sex, she had climaxed more than she ever had in her life, making it impossible to believe that he was still erect and going strong.

Looking over her shoulder, Monya wiped her sweat-drenched hair out of her face and glared at Supreme through slits. Biting on her bottom lip to keep from screaming, she wondered if maybe this was all just a dream. Was it actually possible that she had found a well-endowed man with the skills to make her body melt, and have him be paid?

Unable to stay on her hands and knees any longer due to the earthquake climax that suddenly ripped through her middle, she collapsed on her stomach, screaming, "I'm cumming! Oh God, I'm cumming, baby!"

Continuing his pounding as her body violently trembled beneath him, Supreme concluded that his job had been completed by the sounds of her now weak moans that bordered on the edge of being painful cries. Reaching forward to remove her long, soaked hair from her face, he leaned over her prone back and rose up in a manner that allowed him to slip out of her tight wetness. Lying on top of her back with his erection resting between her abundant cheeks, he gently kissed her neck before asking, "Are you alright, beautiful?"

Feeling as if a long awaited weight had been lifted from her body, Monya found comfort in the closeness she now felt as she lay flat on her stomach with her legs spread wide, and Supreme resting on top of her. Turning her head to look him straight in the eye, she replied, "I don't think I've ever been better. Now, how about telling me what exactly you just did to me?" she questioned with a sly grin.

Returning her grin, Supreme responded, "Did to you, you say?" Raising an eyebrow in suspense, he spoke in a flat, sincere tone, "I just gave you what I knew you needed." Massaging one of her breasts, he added, "I've wanted to do that ever since I first laid eyes on you. And if you have no objections, I'm not finished."

In surprise, Monya raised an eyebrow at the force of his unexpected change of position that forced her on her side. Feeling his erection sliding back into position to enter her, she raised her leg and threw it over his. Closing her eyes, the last thought that entered her mind as he began to wedge himself into her body was, "Please, forgive me, Chez!"

Dressed in all black, Boo-Boo blended into the dark scenery around him easily. Ready for warfare, he wore a bulletproof vest, because even though he had come to kill, there was always a chance that he too would have to wear some slugs to accomplish his mission. Understanding that to get caught slipping in the center of 5th Ward was a death sentence, he had no qualms with murdering whoever crossed his path. Therefore, he gripped the forty-five he now held much tighter as he patiently awaited his prey.

Out of bounds or not, until he punished Ice properly, Boo-Boo prepared to brave the cold however long it took for the nigga to exit the house. Noticing how packed the gambling house actually was, he found himself checking the distance between himself and the car that sat only twenty feet away, and the house that stood nearly double that distance from Ice's Volvo.

Biding his time, there was no doubt in Boo-Boo's mind that he had Ice exactly where he wanted him. Even with the vast number of 5th Ward dudes who were inside the house, he felt that no amount of assistance they could offer their comrade would be enough to keep him out of hell. This, Boo-Boo was confident of, because he was prepared to die in order to ensure it.

Checking the time on his watch, Ice tossed back his drink and frowned at the burning sensation of the alcohol as it traveled down his throat. Already drunk, he set the empty cup down and scanned the room in an attempt to see if anything caught his eyes that was worthy of accompanying him home. Finding nothing but a roomful of hood rats, he snubbed his nose at the choices, thinking that he would rather go home alone than take any of them.

Grabbing his money from the crap table with one hand and his gun with the other, he said, "I'm out, fellows." Receiving an array of parting words, he placed his gun in the small of his back and headed towards the exit.

Hearing his name being called, Ice stopped short of reaching the door and turned to the voice. Spotting Moon sitting in the corner, smoking a blunt, Ice gave him a questioning stare.

Exhaling a cloud of smoke, Moon asked, "Where you heading to, player?"

Never one to give up unnecessary answers, Ice asked, "Why? What you need?"

"I need a ride downtown if you can swing it, homie."

Reaching for the offered blunt, Ice replied, "If you got more of this good smelling tree, you got a ride, nigga."

Winking his already partially closed eye in a somewhat conspiratorial manner, Moon responded, "That's not a problem. I got too much of this." Releasing the blunt, he said, "Let me grab my coat and I'll be right with you, man."

Heading for the door with Moon's blunt hanging from the corner of his mouth, Ice boasted, "If you can't find me, I'll be in the Volvo with the knocking ass system."

"Bingo!" Boo-Boo mumbled in a low tone at the sight of Ice exiting the house with a blunt in his mouth. Awaiting Ice's next move, he whispered, "I got your ass now, nigga!"

Recalling the amount of money he'd lost at the crap table, Ice took a deep draw on the blunt, then tossed it in the bushes as he stepped from the porch and headed towards his car. Though he hated to lose, money was his least worry, with all the cocaine that Supreme had brought to town.

Strolling in his careless way of walking, Ice felt a mysterious presence behind him that couldn't be mistaken. Slowly turning to investigate, he chuckled in a menacing manner at what he saw behind him. "Yo, what the hell is this?" he questioned, laughing even harder. "You're joking, right?"

Realizing that the masked figure hadn't lowered the forty-fives that were trained on his chest, Ice's laughter immediately stopped to be replaced by an ice grill that left no doubt of his monstrous nature. Staring through blood red slits, he growled in a high pitch, "Bitch, nigga, apparently you don't know who the fuck I am!" Pounding his fist against his chest in a rage, he spat, "I'm Ice, and you're buying yourself a death warrant by fucking with me, motherfucker!"

Laughing in a sarcastic manner, Boo-Boo held Ice with the same furious glare that was reflected in Ice's eyes as he slowly raised the mask to allow Ice his first and last glimpse of who really stood before him.

Seeing the instant change that came upon Ice's features at the recognition of the enemy behind the mask, Boo-Boo sneered, "You were wrong, nigga. I know exactly who I'm fucking with." Noticing the way Ice unconsciously looked around for an escape route, Boo-Boo said, "Fuck you, you faggot ass nigga! When you killed my cousin, you signed your own death certificate!"

No sooner than the mask had raised and Ice saw Boo-Boo's face, he realized how serious the situation really was. Knowing that Boo-Boo was a cold murderer and it didn't seem like Moon would arrive in time, Ice didn't plan on going out without a fight. Going for the weapon that sat in the small of his back, the only thought that raced through his mind was kill or be killed. Then, he felt the first round rip through his thick leather coat and explode in his chest.

Seeing the first slug rip into Ice's upper chest, Boo-Boo ran up on him with the two four-fifths flaming. Slamming Ice's body against the Volvo with an explosive volley of slugs, he stood over him in a killing rage, watching blood, brains and guts explode from the mutilated jerking body. Realizing that he was already dead, Boo-Boo still walked up on the lifeless body and placed two more rounds into Ice's head. Watching them tear through what was left of his head, embedding themselves in the car door, he smiled at the rising smoke that surrounded Ice's burning hair.

Bringing Boo-Boo's exciting moment to an end, he was thrown forward with the force of the slug that slammed into his back.

Witnessing what was happening to Ice in a state of shock, Moon quickly pulled his own weapon and began to fire at Ice's attacker as he ran down the steps in an attempt to save him. Catching him completely by surprise, Moon saw the black clad figure stumble and go down.

Trying to fight the pain, Boo-Boo cursed himself for allowing someone to catch him off guard, as he rolled beneath Ice's Volvo to take cover. Gritting his teeth to block out the pain, he took aim and fired both weapons at the reckless figure that was running towards him with his own gun blazing.

Dropping him in his tracks with a barrage of slugs, Boo-Boo jumped up from where he had been taking cover beneath the Volvo and began to run, knowing that it wouldn't be long before a small army of their homies would arrive to join the battle. Thinking that he would return to finish the battle another day, he moved through the alleyways as quickly as his injured body would take him as the loud, alarmed voices faded in the distance.

Critically wounded, Moon lay in the middle of the street with blood pouring from his mouth. Rambling on in a completely inaudible manner due to the wracking coughs that made his words impossible to decipher, his partner, Fonzo, lowered his ear closer to his mouth so that he could hear what it was that Moon was trying to tell him.

Continuing to cough as his eyes rolled back in his head, Moon slowly began to whisper, "It… was… Boo-Boo… who did… this… man. Boo-Boo… from 3rd Ward," he wheezed.

About to question Moon further, even though the name he gave said it all, Fonzo looked in his face and shook his head at the eyes that he encountered, which were frozen in time.

The looks that passed amongst the group of angry soldiers said it all. Two of their homies were gone, and there was nothing that they could do to bring them back. Yet, what their eyes also said was that the shit was about to hit the fan in a major way, and after the events of the night, nothing could alter the course that had been set.

Strutting in the house and kicking off her heels, Monya made it no further than the living room before she dropped down on the plush loveseat. She was dead tired, but satisfied beyond belief. Wincing in pain as she stretched her legs out in front of her, it dawned on her that she had never experienced anything comparable to what Supreme had done to her tonight. Even the pain she now felt in her center due to the no less than eleven inches she had gone up against, couldn't even compete with the pleasure that his sweet punishment had produced.

Dreamily allowing her mind to travel through the events of the night, she couldn't believe that she had actually given her body to another man. Up to this point, Chez had been her first and only lover. However, after experiencing the memorable talents of Supreme's exceptional loving, she found herself wondering why she had waited so long.

Nevertheless, regardless of how long she had waited, Monya refused to continue being alone. Although she still loved Chez with all her heart and had no intentions of leaving him, she would gladly allow Supreme to take up his slack in the bedroom when needed.

Sighing in relief, Monya exclaimed, "I'll never be stupid or blind to you and your ways again, Chez!" Closing her eyes and leaning further into the comfort of the cushioned chair, she couldn't help thinking that from this moment on, things would more than likely never be the same again.

Immediately confronted with the murders of Ice and Moon upon returning home, Supreme found the enjoyment he had been experiencing at the thought of making passionate love to Monya put on hold. Wondering to himself how such a beautiful night could end on the messed up note that he now saw his own becoming, he rubbed his temples in disbelief as he watched Mann stalk around the room like a caged animal.

Answering his own question, he figured that none of this would be happening if Mann, Dax and Ice hadn't made the foolish mistake of taking it upon themselves to run out and murder Satin a few months earlier. Now, it seemed that by whatever means, Boo-Boo had uncovered the proof of their involvement. With that being the case, no one involved would be safe from Chez's whole crew. Realizing what that meant, Supreme concluded that it was about to get real nasty, real soon.

Pacing the floor in a rage, Mann came to an abrupt stop and loudly proclaimed, "I'm gonna kill that motherfucker in the worst way!" As if in a daze, he spat, "Just you wait and see, Ice! I'm not allowing his ass to get away with this shit!"

Looking around the room, Supreme shook his head at the careless looks that were plastered on the faces of Dax, Unique and

Rio as they all but ignored Mann's performance.

No longer in the mood for games, Supreme stared in Mann's direction with an angry glare that quickly got his attention. "What the fuck is wrong with you, nigga? This shit ain't a game." Glancing from Mann to the rest of the people, he snapped, "As I speak, I'm willing to wager that Boo-Boo and his crew are having the same conversation about us. They're not going to wait for us to strike back. The element of surprise we once had at our disposal is over. Now, I can't tell the rest of you how you should carry it, but I know that it's on, and I'm not going to be sitting around here unprepared for their arrival."

Peering into the faces that surrounded him, Supreme could tell by the mean looks that emanated from their features that they were in agreement with him. Turning to face Mann's defiant glare, he gave the first official command that would solidify his position as their leader.

"We have a short period of time to make a lot of decisions that may make the difference between our people living or dying, so sit down and listen."

Holding Supreme in a staring battle, Mann, even in his angry state, knew that the war between their two sides was inevitable at this point. Deciding that Supreme spoke the truth and they needed to be ready, Mann slowly complied with his wishes and took a seat.

Smiling inwardly at Mann's unconscious release of power to him, Supreme concluded that maybe tonight's events hadn't been such a bad thing after all. With Monya in the bag and the leaders of 5th Ward prepared to follow his lead in the upcoming war, he could truly say that everything had fallen into place exactly as he had planned.

Awakening from the continuous knocking on the door, I rolled from beneath Aneesa's sleeping form, pulled on my boxers and went to see what was happening. Opening the door, ready to confront whoever had awakened me, I was met by Qwen, Sam and Dresser, who were fully dressed with grim looks plastered on their faces. Stepping aside to allow them entrance, I exhaled, "You three aren't here banging on my door this early for no reason, so what's wrong?"

"Boo-Boo's been shot!" Qwen angrily announced, getting straight to the point.

Suddenly wide-awake, I yelled, "What?" before asking, "How bad is it, man?"

Dropping down on the couch with a faraway look pasted on his face, Qwen replied, "He's alright. He was wearing a vest." Locking eyes with me, he nonchalantly added, "Shit is about to get real wicked back home, bro. Boo-Boo says he murdered Ice and put slugs up in the kid, Moon as well. He wasn't able to tell me if Moon made it or not because he was forced to make a quick exit."

Thinking that as long as my partner was safe, I couldn't care less who died. My only question was, "Why did he murder Ice though?"

Breaking our eye contact, Qwen sighed and stared off into the distance. "The word is, Ice, Dax and Mann were the ones responsible for killing Satin."

Getting my undivided attention with his last statement, it was clear to me why they were fully dressed. The vacation was over. Snapping out orders as I turned to storm back into the room, I informed, "We're going home, so someone call and make our reservations."

Dressing in a hurry, I heard Aneesa turn over. "Where you going, Chez?" she asked.

"Home," I responded flatly as I continued to dress.

Covering her nakedness, she watched me move around the room in quiet contemplation before asking, "Is everything alright, papi?"

"Uh-hmm," was my only reply, being that my mind was crowded with a million different thoughts, and holding a conversation with her at this point just didn't fit into the equation.

Refusing to accept my change of attitude, Aneesa sat up in bed, allowed the covers to fall freely from her naked frame, and spoke in a seductive, sultry tone, "When will I see you again, Chez?"

Stopping what I was doing, I gave her a look filled with irritation, then blurted out, "Write your number down, give it to me, and I'll call you, alright?"

Watching her reach for a pad and pen on the nightstand, I could tell that she wasn't used to being given the cold shoulder. She was beautiful, and as she wrote down her digits, her deliciously thick lips were poked out in a pout. But, due to the abrupt change of plans, she had become nothing more than another beauty who would more than likely never hear from me again.

Reaching for the number while leaning down to suckle her full lips between my own, I laid a thin pile of Benjamin's on the nightstand that would surely make up for my unexpected departure. Breaking our lip embrace, I turned and snatched up my single piece of luggage, saying, "I'll be in contact." I then headed through the door without another glance in her direction.

Leaning back in my seat, I felt the plane taxiing down the runway. Making our way home, I couldn't necessarily speak for my partners who, like myself, were wrapped up in their own thoughts, but I, on the other hand, couldn't wait to return so that I could pay my respects to the motherfucker who had murdered my man. After being calm for a long time and listening to the old timers' rule that stated 'Getting money and committing murder just didn't mix,' I was prepared to re-emerge. Now that my money was long, I could easily switch up my game plan and send a few unlucky niggas to hell.

Whether Mann and Dax where aware of it or not, I had no idea. But, thanks to them, the old Chez had returned, and I was coming with a team of warriors by my side. The two of them were already dead as far as I was concerned, but no one around them was safe either. In fact, I figured that their whole side of the city would be held responsible as well.

Chuckling low, but in no way finding the slightest humor in my thoughts, I wondered if they were really ready for war.

Chapter 16

Unable to sleep since receiving the call from Chez in the middle of the night, Neeta had reluctantly hauled her young, rather sexy conquest of the evening out of the bed and sent him packing. Hating to see him leave after all the pleasurable moments they had shared earlier, she concluded that as long as all her bills and monetary needs were taken care of by Chez, she would never leave him hanging. This was why she now sat in the Lexus, awaiting his return as he instructed.

Feeling the weight of his .40-calibor pistol tucked inside her purse, she couldn't help wondering what the urgency in his voice had been about. Thinking that it really wasn't her business, she stared out at the traffic and people that were busily moving around her, before coming to the conclusion that she had been sitting double parked in a fire lane entirely too long.

Sighing loudly, Neeta rolled her eyes and raised the sleeve on her leather coat to check the time on her newly purchased Cartier watch. Slumping back into the butter-soft leather interior with a slight pout plastered on her features due to having to wait so long, she slowly allowed a sly smile to replace her pout.

In all honesty, she had no reason to do anything but smile, because she had it going on. Chez took care of her well, and at the age of 21, she was living the life of the rich and famous. With diamonds glimmering on each of her fingers and both of her wrists, a fly ass Lexus, and one of the biggest houses in her exclusive suburb, Neeta knew that she was the shit. Yet, the little she now possessed was no match for what she would have once Monya was out of the way and Chez belonged to her alone. With that thought in mind, she exclaimed, "It won't be long now, bitch!"

Strolling through the airport, we ignored the many stares that followed us as we passed. With the jewels and furs we wore, they really couldn't help their staring, but we couldn't have cared one way or the other. In a nutshell, we had much more important matters on our minds.

Exiting the airport, I stopped and stared around me before catching sight of Neeta's baby blue Lexus parked up ahead. Turning to face my crew, I said, "I've got some business I have to attend to before we meet up tonight, fellows. But I'll give you each a call later."

After reaching out and giving me pounds, they began to walk away. At the last moment, I instructed, "Lay as low as possible. We don't want our enemies, or anyone else for that matter, to know that we've returned, alright?"

Although Dresser and Sam nodded their heads in acknowledgment of my statement, Qwen stopped and turned to face me. "You just be careful on your end, bro. We got this," he said with a grin as he backpedaled towards Sam's waiting 7-Series Beamer.

Heading towards Neeta as I watched them walk away, the thought that members of my own crew may have to die when the war was set in motion came to mind. Wanting to ensure their safety, but knowing that it wasn't possible to do so, I concluded that whatever the end result was, I had no control over fate.

Neeta excitedly jumped from the car and threw her arms around his neck and planted a kiss on his lips.

"Hey, baby! How was your trip, boo?" She strutted around to the passenger side of the vehicle, thinking of just how lucky she was to have his fine, paid ass gone over her.

Jumping in the driver's seat, Chez adjusted the seat.

"My trip was alright, baby."

Whipping the Lexus into traffic, I glanced over at her and smiled at the way she was curled up in the seat, looking all sexy. Reaching a hand out to caress her long, dark hair, I said, "Guess what, boo? I'm gonna need to camp out at your spot for a few days."

Forcing a smile, Neeta wanted to scream out, Oh no you're not either! Instead, she said, "Oh yeah? Well, I'm not going to ask what I owe the pleasure of your company to, because anything that allows me to spend time with you is just fine by me."

Remembering what my instructions to her had been, I asked, "Did you bring my joint, baby?"

Choosing to let her actions speak for her, Neeta reached inside her purse and removed the big weapon. Grabbing an extra clip out of her pocket, she handed them both to me.

Turning the volume on her system up as I placed the gun on my waist, I began to plan a strategy in my mind that would go into effect no sooner than darkness arrived. Staring ahead expressionless,

I vowed to make tonight a night that their crew would never forget.

After taking a shower and changing clothes, I took a chance that I wouldn't normally have taken, and called Monique. Receiving a much better outlook on exactly what I was up against, I was glad that I had contacted her. Being from the 5th Ward, any questions coming from her wouldn't be seen as unusual, and that's what I had counted on. Therefore, when she called back with the information that Mann was rolling with a New Yorker named Supreme, who the grapevine said was moving major weight, I decided right then that she would be compensated well for her time. What made her even more invaluable was the fact that she had gone one step further for me and found out where two of their stash houses were located.

With that knowledge, I was ready to hit them where it would hurt the most—their pockets. Even though we were murdering whoever we found in their spots, if by chance we were able to catch the big targets, we would just be killing two birds with one stone.

Dressed in my all black creep gear from head to toe, I was ready. Making one last check of the weapons I had slung underneath my arms in specially made holsters, I snatched the keys to Neeta's old Honda off the counter. Heading towards the door, I was glad that I had tinted her windows, painted it black and kept it for purposes such as this. Closing the door behind me, it was obvious that everything was in order. Now, all that was left to do was meet up with my dogs, who were waiting and ready to set it off.

Arriving at the rendezvous spot, I found that my crew was in attendance. They were each dressed in all black and sporting stone faces. Scanning them closely as I exited the car, I was immediately alarmed by what I saw in Dresser's eyes. It was crystal clear that Sam, Boo-Boo and Qwen were prepared, but I realized that Dresser wasn't cut out for the murder game, so I made a decision on the spot. "Okay, fellows, there's been a change of plans." Staring directly at Dresser,

I noticed him nervously darting his eyes around as if wishing for an escape route. "I'm taking Sam with me. Qwen and Boo-Boo have the other house." Narrowing my eyes as I glanced at Dresser, I coolly stated with a level of disgust mixed with understanding, "You sit this one out."

As expected, I saw him release a relieved sigh, along with a remnant of a smile that he seemed to be struggling with all of his might to hold on to. Cutting my eyes in the direction of the others, I could somewhat gauge that they understood my reasoning. Yet, it was the blank expression that went along with Qwen's slight head nod that let me know that I had made the correct decision. "Alright everyone, come on over so we can go over this."

Leaning against the Honda, I slowly laid out a step by step format as to how we would pull off our heists. Finishing up, I surveyed each of their faces for questions. Finding none, I said, "Tonight, we'll be sending these niggas a message that they can't possibly miss." Locking eyes with my crew, I spoke in a voice so strong and direct that it couldn't be mistaken. "I want no one in the houses to be breathing when we leave. Even the dog catches slugs. Be careful, and give me a call as soon as you two finish." Turning to get in the car with Sam by my side, I heard my name being called and turned my head towards the voice.

Almost to their own car, Qwen slowed his gait. "Be careful, and don't take any unnecessary chances, you hear me, bro?" he said.

Ducking my head to enter the car, I confidently boasted, "I'll be just fine, D. If anything, you need to be worried about the niggas who have to see me tonight!" Laughing as I pulled off, I meant every word, and then some.

Excited at the sight of the big AMG Benz with New York plates that sat in front of the house, I had no doubt that we hit the lotto with Monique's information. Estimating that the whip ran around one-hundred thousand, I figured that at such a high price tag, just maybe I would get lucky enough to find Supreme inside the house. Hitting the lights as we pulled to a stop a few houses down, I anxiously turned to Sam and asked, "You ready, dog?"

Pushing a cartridge into the black pistol grip pump that rested on his lap, he flatly responded, "Hell yeah. Let's handle our business, my nigga."

Knowing he was a veteran who could more than hold his own, I popped the door and said, "Let's do it then." I exited the car at a slow crouch.

Hugging the shadows, we made it to the back of the house. Listening to make sure that no one had been alerted to our arrival, I slowly raised up to where I could look through what I found to be the kitchen window. Through a gap in the curtains, I was able to make out two men who, from what I could see, were busy counting piles of money. Taking a further look around, I saw a stack of packaged, white, clear wrapped keys. Even though I had not laid eyes on any weapons, I realized that the possibility of them actually sitting around all of that money and coke without protection was foolish. The artillery couldn't have been too far away.

Crouching back down, I whispered to Sam, "I'm going through the back door. As soon as you hear my foot connect with the door, start blasting through the windows. We got them in the middle of counting their dough, and I spotted a pile of bricks on the counter." Smiling wickedly, I said, "This shit is going to be real easy, player. Just make sure that they don't have a chance to get their shit together."

Moving past him, I saw the pump being raised towards the window as he replied, "I'll make sure to keep them real busy."

Reaching the back door, I slowly removed the twin .40-cals from their holsters, took in a deep breath and slammed my black

Timberland into the doorknob with all the force I could muster. Watching splinters fly from the doorframe as it caved inwards, I heard the first blasts from the riot pump.

Entering the chaotic scene with the .40's releasing their own trails of flames, I saw one of the men who had been in the process of reaching for his burner catch a shotgun blast in the stomach. It sent him and the chair he was sitting in, flying into a cabinet.

Turning just in time to see the other coming up out of his chair with what looked to be a nine, I cut both barrels loose on him. Watching huge chunks of bloody flesh fly from what used to be his face, the dead weight of his body crashed loudly onto the table before crumbling to the floor.

Glimpsing Sam as he entered and slid past me to check the rest of the house, I frowned distastefully at the blood, guts and slimy brain matter that dripped from the kitchen table into puddles on the floor. Staring around me, I found the same gore dripping from the walls and counters, but the book bag was what I was really interested in. Grabbing it, I quickly began to pack the wet money and cocaine inside.

It was funny, but out of nowhere the thought came to me that all my life, drug money had been referred to as "blood money". For once, the statement literally held true, because the money was soaked with it.

Handing the bag to Sam, who had just returned from his short search, I shot an amused glance at the lifeless bodies that lay strewn around me. Drawing an identity from what was left of one of them, I found that even with the half a face that the second one wearing the large diamond charm around his neck had left, I still couldn't recall ever seeing him before.

"Come on!" Sam snapped before loudly adding, "The police can't be far behind!"

"I'm coming," I lied, choosing instead to step closer to the unidentified dead man. Bending over, I reached down and ripped the chain and diamond charm from his neck and wiped it on his pants leg to remove the blood that covered the inscription. "Rio, huh? Now, who the hell are you Rio?" Smiling at the thought of actually having a conversation with a dead man, I placed the chain in my pocket and figured that whoever he had once been, he was no more than a dead man at this point.

It was only as I walked out of the door that it came to me exactly whose chain rested in my pocket. Rio was one of the men who was in the Range the day I knocked Mann out. Adding an extra level of excitement to a night that was already turning out to be rather exciting already, I loved the fact that we had not only murdered one of their flunkies and made off with their shit, but we had struck them a brutal blow by murdering one of their own.

Blending into the shadows, it was clear that our portion of the mission had been a success. I couldn't help but wonder how the other half of my crew was making out.

Speedily exiting the stash house, Boo-Boo and Qwen carried a substantial amount of drugs and money along with them. Neither spoke, but the silence in itself was proof enough that they were in no way happy about the fact that one of the two bodies they had left behind for the maggots to feast on was a female.

In deep thought, Qwen couldn't help battling with the idea that had he left her alive, somewhere down the line he would live to regret the decision. Knowing the female, the only question that continued to eat at him was, Why did she have to pick tonight to come give the nigga some ass? Concluding that whether she was cool or not, she had seen their faces, so the way it had gone down was just the way it was meant to be.

Arriving at the car and getting inside, his features suddenly became cold as he dialed Chez's number with the thought of the other murder of the night on his mind. With no sorrow whatsoever, Qwen relived the ease of standing over Chuck and releasing a whole clip into his bucking body.

Hearing Chez say, "What's good?" on the other end of the receiver, his last thoughts were, Fuck that nigga! because, he had no doubt that if the tables had been turned, Chuck would have gladly done the same to him.

Snapping out of it, Qwen said, "The mission's complete, and it went off without a hitch." Cutting his eyes at Boo-Boo, he was met with an expressionless glance. "How did everything go on your end, bro?"

"We're good. Real good, as a matter of fact." Against discussing our business over the phone, he said, "I'll see you at the spot."

Ending the call with Qwen, I grinned at Sam. "The shit went off like clockwork, nigga."

Nodding his head with a shadow of a smile pasted on his features, Sam's only response was, "I never doubted that it would, player."

Reaching the spot only seconds after Qwen and Boo-Boo, I couldn't help but to notice the two big bags they carried. It suddenly became clear to me that like ourselves, they had come up tonight.

Glancing back, they opened the door and headed inside the house as we exited the car. Entering close behind, I hit the numerous bolts that secured our spot, and took the steps three at a time in my eagerness to find out exactly what we had made off with.

Walking in last, I was utterly surprised at the sight that greeted me. Loudly exclaiming, "Whew!" I stared at the stacks of money that were sliding off the glass table and forming new piles on the floor. Unable to believe that they had actually been careless enough to let us walk right in and take what I decided was a few hundred thousand, I exploded into laughter when I noticed the many bricks of coke they were busy removing from the other two bags.

Chuckling as well, Boo-Boo sarcastically stated, "Now those bitches get a chance to see how hot we can make it!"

"Hot!" Sam said, laughing menacingly. "Player, they have no idea how much hotter we're about to make shit for them."

Taking notice of how quiet Qwen was as he sat down, lit a blunt and began to count the money, I knew that something was on his mind. Reaching out to grab a stack myself, I decided that it wasn't my place to question him. He would discuss it when he was ready. So for now, I'd let it ride and count our newfound riches instead.

Cradling the phone against her ear, Monya lay on her stomach with a bright smile plastered on her face.

"Baby, you realize that I'm missing you like mad, right?" Supreme questioned in a low, lust-filled voice.

Thinking that she would love for him to be able to show her how much he really missed her, Monya twirled a long strand of curls around her finger and replied, "As much as I'm missing you, I sure hope that you're feeling the same."

Deciding that Chez's silly ass had been too busy chasing tricks in the street to notice that his own woman was in need of attention, Supreme concluded that after only one night of slinging his good dick, she was sprung. Smiling at the thought that Chez didn't have a chance against him now that he had placed his hooks in Monya, he figured that he would see just how far she was prepared to go for him.

"I'm laying here with my eyes closed, and I have a vivid picture of you in my head," he announced, hitting the Backwood he held. Blowing out a cloud of fragrant smoke, he asked, "What are you wearing, baby?"

Immediately feeling her body heat up as her nipples hardened to the sound of his voice alone, Monya shuddered, "I'm... uh... I'm... wearing a pair of..." she swallowed, "French cut panties and a short lace T-shirt. "Why... do... you ask?" she stammered.

Umm, he thought, closing his eyes for real this time at the slowly rising pressure in his middle due to the mental picture he conjured up of her in the panties and lace T-shirt. "I wonder if you'll do me a favor and slide up out of those panties. There's something I want you to do for me."

"Umm, baby, you're bad!" Monya laughed in a teasing manner. Lowering her voice to merely a whisper, she asked, "What is it you want me to do for you?"

"Well, let's start by—" Damn! he thought as the clicking of his other line interrupted their conversation. "Hold on a moment, ma. I have to get this." Clicking over, he irritably snapped, "What?"

"We've got problems!" Mann angrily stated.

Just as angrily, Supreme asked, "What problems do we have now, Mann?"

Sighing heavily, Mann replied, "Two of our stash houses were hit hard tonight, man. None of our people who were inside them were spared." Lowering his tone, Mann spoke with a voice that dripped with sorrow. "Cuz, Rio was murdered in one of the houses!"

Jumping up from the couch in disbelief, Supreme threw the phone against the wall and watched it shatter into numerous pieces. In a fury, he screamed, "No! Not my family!"

Waiting for Neeta to exit the shower, I lay in bed with my arms comfortably resting behind my head, reliving the night's events. Unable to relinquish the thoughts of just how good it felt to take a nigga's shit, I couldn't contain the smile that lit up my face at the realization of us actually making off with over 300-grand and 14 keys in one night.

Allowing my eyes to wander towards the dresser and diamond encrusted charm that was connected to the chain on top of it, my smile intensified. Even more than the money and drugs we had taken, the chain was the trophy I was the proudest of. With it came the satisfaction that someone as close to their crew as Satin had been to me and mine, had been murdered by my hand. That alone supplied me with the satisfaction I longed for.

"You ready for me, baby?" Neeta questioned with a sly grin on her face, while the only thing that covered her wet body was a small towel.

Forgetting my previous thoughts of being satisfied, I suddenly found myself in need of a more pleasurable form of satisfaction as I stared through lust filled eyes at the perfection that stood before me. Locking my eyes with hers, I slowly removed the covers from my nakedness, allowing my protruding erection to answer for me.

Lowering her eyes to my midsection, her mouth opened in an involuntary gasp at what bobbed excitedly before her. Immediately dropping the towel, Neeta said, "My fault. I forgot about the no clothes rule." Walking towards me in a seductive manner, she smiled deviously before adding, "I thrive to follow the rules, baby." Reaching for the lengthy erection as she slithered across the bed on her stomach, she positioned it only inches from her gloss coated lips. Cutting her eyes in my direction, she whispered, "Rule number one, and the most important of all is, I'll never leave you hanging, Chez." Proving her point, she slowly allowed her lips to devour my length.

Watching her through narrowed eyes, I concluded that this was a night to remember for all times. At that very moment, I decided that I was untouchable.

Chapter 17

Though Supreme stood straight and regal, what he now found himself viewing was without question the hardest thing he had ever done. Feeling as if Rio's death was his responsibility, he had been battling with his conscience, wishing that he had never brought him down South in the beginning. Now, after only 24 years on Earth, the cousin, whom he had never been far from their whole lives, was dead. Having to present Rio's body to his mother had torn his heart to shreds.

From where he stood, apart from the rest of the mourners, Supreme watched Rio's casket being lowered into the ground with unblinking eyes, as the rain poured over him in blinding sheets. Although he was drenched, it made no difference, because the rain only helped to disguise the tears that flowed in an unbridled torrent down his face.

Glancing at his aunt through tear filled eyes as she sat slumped over in grief, he silently vowed that his cousin wouldn't die alone.

With coat in hand, Supreme stared across the expanse that separated him from the last glance of Rio's disappearing casket. Whispering in a low tone, he said, "Your death will only be the beginning of a lot more bloodshed. I love you, man, and we will meet again." Having given his final farewell, he strolled towards the car, with Unique and Mann following close on his heels.

Exiting the cemetery in Supreme's black 560 Benz, Mann answered his phone and spoke in a low tone. Hanging up, he turned to Supreme and spoke in the same manner. "I think we've found out how they got the information on our houses, cuz."

Momentarily holding Mann's stare, Supreme asked, "How?"

"The word is the bitch, Monique, was asking around about us and our business right before the shit went down."

Rising from his reclining position, Supreme's face twisted into an angry mask. "Monique? Who the fuck is a Monique, Mann?"

"She's a little dimepiece from around the way whose man was down with us at one time. The nigga's doing a bid at the moment though."

"Oh yeah!" Supreme snapped. "Well, if we find out that this Monique bitch had anything to do with our houses getting hit, her ass is history, and your homie won't have a damn girl!"

Leaning back in his seat, Supreme's mind was running wild. In deep thought, the only thing he was sure of was that Chez and his crew had been involved. Deciding right then that he wanted the pleasure of murdering Chez himself, he concluded that the time for games and patience had ended. As far as he was concerned, when they killed Rio, all-out war had begun. Now, he would have to show them how it was done when you're really at war.

Ready to take the ultimate step in her plot to have Chez completely to herself, Neeta rehearsed the words she planned to say over and over in her head. Somewhat nervous now that the time had arrived, she was aware that the whole idea could possibly explode in her face if she had somehow underestimated the extent of Chez's love for her versus the love he held for Monya. Biting her bottom lip as she paced from one wall of her large bedroom to the other, she juggled her options, then rethought them.

Realizing that she possessed everything she ever wanted and more, Neeta poked her lips out in a pout as it dawned on her that none of it was important if she was only second best. It wasn't so much the fact that she wanted Chez, per se. It was more that she was tired of being the other woman. Monya held the position that she now envisioned for herself—the number one position.

Making up her mind, Neeta decided that regardless of the end result, it was a go. She would call Monya, lay her relationship with Chez out on the table, and allow the cards to fall wherever they landed. Glancing towards the phone with an evil grin in place, she concluded that it was all or nothing.

Making up for lost time, we sold the coke that we'd taken from the New York clown and his crew. Clearing over 800-thousand between the 14 bricks we had sold and the loot we took, the 300-grand I'd taken for myself was sitting comfortably in the safe I had installed in Neeta's house for a rainy day.

Although the bulk of my money was safely buried in airtight canisters, I had also placed a safe in my home that contained over a million dollars as well. Trusting Monya over all others, I gave her the combination for emergency purposes, but she had no idea just how much was inside.

Thinking of Monya and her loyalty throughout the years, I realized that as soon as our beef was dealt with, I would do something real special for her. On further thought, I decided that a month in the Caribbean would do the trick.

Smiling at the thought of my lady, myself and nothing but the sea, white sand and the blue skies to keep us company, gave me the urge to hear her sexy voice. Grabbing the phone, I began to dial her number.

Pacing back and forth through the house, Monya couldn't quite seem to get herself together. Unable to understand why she hadn't heard from Supreme since their last conversation over a week ago, it irritated her that even after paging him numerous times today, he still hadn't returned her call.

Hating to second-guess her actions, she started to wonder whether she had made a mistake by having a one-night stand with him in the first place. Beginning to feel worse with the knowledge that she may have played herself, she wondered how something that felt so good could possibly have her feeling so down now.

Forgetting the question as she raced to grab the ringing phone that had to be Supreme, Monya felt her heart skip a beat.

"Hey, baby!" she said, snatching the phone up in mid-ring. "Where are you?" she questioned excitedly.

Laughing, Chez replied, "If you must know, I'm making my rounds through the city. But what have I done to receive such a pleasant reaction from you today, baby?"

At the sound of Chez's voice instead of Supreme's, all excitement drained from her features, immediately replacing her smile with a frown. Taking a moment to answer his question due to not wanting the displeasure in her voice to be heard, she cleared her throat and gave a strained laugh. "You didn't do anything but catch me lying here resting, baby."

Smiling at the thought of just how much rest he had planned for the two of them real soon, Chez said, "Look, baby. I know I haven't been spending much time with you lately. That's going to change, I promise." Sighing, he spoke with sincerity, "I've been slacking in this relationship, and even though I don't tell you as much as I should, I love you with all my heart, Monya."

Biting her lip as she listened to the sweetest words she had heard him speak in ages, she felt the tears beginning to well up in her eyes as she stated, "I love you even more, baby." Yet, even though that was the case, she wished that he had made his declaration before she had slept with Supreme. Wanting to make love to her man and forget her one and only indiscretion, she said, "When are you coming home, baby? I need you bad."

Feeling like I could use a good long evening of making love to my woman, I said, "I need to run a few more errands, then I'll be right there, alright?"

Hearing the phone click, indicating another call, Monya nervously decided that if it was Supreme, she would make it clear that she wanted nothing else to do with him, and forget that there had ever been anything between them, regardless of how hard it was to do so.

"I'm gonna answer the phone, but hurry home, boo." Clicking over, she whispered, "Hello."

"And hello to you, Ms. Monya!" the arrogant female voice snapped. "Pleasantries aside, I think I should introduce myself. I'm Neeta," she stated with a hint of a smile in her voice. "I'm Chez's other woman." Allowing her words to sink in, she confidently added, "You're going to want to hear the whole story, so please take a seat and allow me to get started."

Dumbfounded, Monya dropped down in a chair with a look of disbelief pasted on her features. Unable to disregard what she immediately knew to be honest words, she mumbled, "I'm sitting."

Talking to his man, Tee, Supreme reached on his hip and removed his pager. Noticing Monya's number once again, he gritted his teeth with the urge to call her back. Unbeknownst to her, not a single day had gone by without her entering his mind. Yet, with the intensity of his business at this point, he couldn't allow anything or anyone to hinder his ability to make the correct decisions. Therefore, regardless of how badly he wanted to be with her, it had to wait.

"Who do you have watching the bitch, Monique?" he questioned while placing his pager back on his hip.

"I got Shawn and Butchy on her, Preme. They won't let her out of their sight," Tee stated matter-of-factly.

Knowing that each of his soldiers were about their business, Supreme truly believed that as Tee stated, she wouldn't be getting out of their sight any time soon.

Bringing a crew of his real New York henchmen—who had come up raw and rugged with him through the years—back after Rio's funeral to ensure that Chez was handled correctly, he had no doubt that he had the upper hand. Receiving an anxious sort of nervous energy at the thought of Chez, he spat, "Who's on Chez?"

"Warren and Ray-Ray are on his tail. Give me the order, and I'll have them murder him right now," Tee exclaimed.

"Nah, money. When the time arrives for him to be dealt with, I'll be the one who puts his ass to sleep." Contemplating doing just that real soon, he ordered, "Keep the tails in place and continue working the phones to let me know their every move."

"Will do, boss. I'll be in contact."

Ending their call, Supreme had a feeling that the long awaited showdown with Chez was imminent.

Excited at the fact that she would soon be meeting with Chez, Monique was in need of the financial boost he had promised to give her. But even more than that, she needed the good gangster loving she planned on receiving before the end of the night. Smiling, she could already imagine the look on his face when he realized that she wore nothing beneath her long leather coat.

Knowing and relishing the fact that her body was her greatest asset, she had always used her thickness to control men. With that particular knowledge in mind, she easily concluded that Chez would be powerless to escape her charms.

Grinning at the thought of getting her way as usual, while whipping through traffic, Monique saw the restaurant where they were to meet, up ahead. Feeling herself beginning to moisten with the wicked thoughts of being intimate, she found herself hoping that he would be on time, because she was in dire need of some physical release.

I wasn't hungry, but since I had decided to bless her, the last thing I needed was to pass off 30-grand in the middle of the street. When it was all said and done, she was just as deep in the mix as the rest of us, and the last thing I wanted was for her to be telling down the line. Even though we had never discussed it, too many people had died for Monique not to have been aware that it was her information that led to their demise. In a hurry to run my other errands and get home to Monya, I made up my mind that the meeting would be handled quickly.

Pulling into the restaurant parking lot, I saw Monique's Hyundai and headed in that direction. Parking the Beamer beside her, I winked my eye and smiled at the cute grin that lit up her beautiful face. Watching her exit the car, I couldn't help staring. She was true dime material, and there was no other way of defining her. The way she strutted in my direction with a pair of thick bow legs that made her look like she had just gotten off a horse had my blood boiling. There was a chance that our meeting could take a little longer than I had originally expected.

Popping the lock on the trunk as I exited the whip, I hugged her, grabbing two hands full of thick, soft ass cheeks before making a quick detour to the trunk. "Have you been here long, ma?" I questioned while eyeing the bag with two keys in the split second it had taken me to deposit my .40-caliber into the trunk.

Hearing her response, but paying little attention to it, I decided to keep my intended schedule. I would quickly conclude my business with her, meet my man, Pooh, with the two keys, and go home to Monya and my daughter.

Closing the trunk and heading towards the restaurant with Monique by my side, it suddenly hit me that I felt naked without my gun. Slowing my steps and looking back at the Beamer, I was tempted to go back and retrieve it, but instead concluded that the last place I needed a gun was the five star restaurant we were heading to.

Listening to Monique's rambling, I couldn't help feeling as though something just wasn't right. The only problem was, I couldn't figure out what it was.

Hanging up the phone, Monya's vision was blurred as she furiously glared around her with unseeing eyes. How this nightmare could be possible after all the years she had struggled alongside him, she would never know. Wanting to believe that Neeta had lied and Chez really planned to tighten up, she wished that she had enough faith in him to do so. Finding that she didn't, it was clear that he did have another, if not many more, women on the side who he lavished luxuries on, and for all she knew, loved. The thought was too much for her to handle, and the racking sobs that shook her body was proof.

Never had Monya's heart ached as much as it did at that moment. What broke her heart the most, was the fact that Neeta had told her of all the things Chez did for her, as well as to her, which were basically the same things he did for her. If he didn't love the bitch, why would he have done those things? she wondered. Unable to answer the one question that would determine whether the relationship she shared with the one man she had loved with all her heart for the last twelve years survived, Monya felt helpless.

No longer prepared to push Supreme away, she had clearly experienced a change of heart. Her heart had been broken for the last time, and she meant to mend it with the love and attention of another. Supreme would help her to repair the pain, and before it was all said and done, Chez would pay for taking her love and loyalty for granted. That, she silently vowed on the life of their child.

"Talk to me." Supreme barked impatiently into his phone.

Listening to Tee's report with an expressionless face, he couldn't believe how good the new turn of events were. It couldn't possibly be this easy, he thought.

"Look," Supreme snapped, cutting Tee off. "We're on our way. Make sure no one moves on him before I arrive."

Hanging up, he turned to Mann with a demonic grin plastered on his face. "It seems that your man's bitch is suspect after all, cuz. They just met up at Constantine's." Removing a chrome .45, he said to himself more so than Mann, "Now I'll have the chance to murder both of them at once."

Glancing sideways at his cousin, Mann could tell by the

menacing grin on his face that he meant to do just what he said. He didn't bother to respond. Right now, all he was interested in was getting to Constantine's so that whatever destiny was in store could be fulfilled.

Having checked the clip, Supreme popped it back in and allowed the memory of Rio's casket being lowered into the ground to come to mind. Becoming even more amped at the thought, he couldn't wait to even the score.

Hard as hell, I no longer had to wonder why Monique hadn't removed her coat when we were seated. Scanning every inch of her perfectly round frame through the open slit in her coat, I had to swallow the saliva that formed in my wide-open mouth.

Spreading her legs further apart to allow me an unobstructed view of her thin, shaved, perfect pink opening, she purred in a voice that dripped with lust, "You like what you see, baby?"

Licking my lips, I responded, "You already know I do, man."

Cutting her eyes at the bulge that strained to escape my pants, she gasped. "We both like what we're seeing then. Look, Chez. Between the sight of that big ol' dick and the 30-grand that's weighing my pockets down, I'm wet and horny as hell." With pleading, lust filled eyes, she asked, "What do you say about us going somewhere and really handling our business, boo?"

Weighing the decision before me, I decided that Pooh could wait another two hours, and I would think of an excuse for Monya later. All I knew at the moment, was that what sat in front of me needed my attention. Tossing enough money on the table to cover our bill, I glanced at my watch, then said, "Let's get out of here."

Fastening her coat, Monique stood and began to lead the way

out of the restaurant. Knowing I would be watching, I enjoyed the extra little twist that she placed in her hips for my benefit.

Chez was unable to see the smile that lingered at the corners of Monique's lips at the thought that she had just gotten her way once again. Thinking devilishly as usual, she realized that real soon she would possess every drop of him. Shuddering at the thought, she decided that they might have to enjoy a quickie before they even left the parking lot. Smiling even brighter, she concluded that a quickie was exactly what she was in need of.

Seeing them as they left the restaurant, Supreme slowly strolled between the parked cars. Thinking that once the two of them were out of the way, he could continue where he and Monya left off, he quickened his steps. Getting closer to his victims, he thought it was funny that Chez was so close to his death and he had no idea that once he no longer existed, his assassin would not only take his life, but everything he owned in the process.

Slowly pulling the hand that held the gun from behind his back, Supreme saw Chez turn away from whatever conversation he was having with Monique, and glance in his direction. Locking eyes with one another for what seemed like an eternity, Supreme saw a glimmer of recognition pass over Chez's features.

Imagining each of the sexual innuendoes Monique was making in the explicit manner that I knew they would take place, I allowed my mind to wander.

Closing her eyes in a state of lust filled bliss, she exclaimed, "I'm so hot, baby!" Leaning into me, she purred, "I just hope you're ready for what I've got in store for you tonight, boy."

Grinning at the hungry look I saw on her face, I palmed her invitingly thick ass. "As far as I'm concerned, you're the one who has problems on your hands, lady."

"Ouch, Chez! Stop, boy!" she jokingly stated with a cute little pout in place. "Your hands are too heavy, and you know you need to be gentle with this good ass."

Thinking to myself that the last thing I planned on doing was being gentle, I said, "Yeah, right! I'm about to punish your ass. Just wait until—"

The words were cut short due to my noticing a stranger walking towards us with a half-smile, half-grimace pasted on his features that just didn't look right. Upon closer inspection, I noticed the chrome pistol slowly appear from behind his back. It was then that I realized what was happening. The gunshots that followed were proof that I had been caught slipping.

In a zone, Supreme saw his first shot find its mark through the center of Chez's chest. Firing the next two slugs into Monique, he watched the look of disbelief cloud her features as she slammed face first into the pavement.

Watching as Chez began to run as if the bullet hadn't fazed him, Supreme sped up to cut off any possible escape. As Supreme ran past Monique's still form, he put another slug in her head. Never taking the time to inspect his work, he knew that there was no chance of her surviving after her cranium exploded into chunks. Raising the big automatic for another shot, he fired and watched as Chez collapsed to the pavement, only to regain his footing and try to escape again. Firing two more rounds into Chez's bullet-ridden body, Supreme decided that there was no way that he would be able to get up again. Running up on him, Supreme was shocked to see that the nigga was still trying to get away.

Watching Chez use one arm to try and drag his body to safety, Supreme stood over his bullet-riddled body and snapped, "Damn, nigga! You ain't trying to make this shit easy for me, are you?"

Unable to escape, Chez stared upwards into the barrel of the raised gun. To Supreme's amazement, he heard the words, "Fuck you, bitch ass nigga! Fire that shit!"

Furious that he had been robbed of the satisfaction of seeing him beg for his life, Supreme fired a wild shot that sent a torrent of blood gushing to the pavement upon contact with Chez's face. Hearing the loud sound of the chamber clacking back at the same moment he heard Tee yelling for him to hurry, Supreme realized that he was out of ammo. Glaring down on Chez's still form, he began to smile as he slowly backed away. Turning to walk off, he boasted, "I'll be sure to take care of your bitch for you, nigga!" Laughing, he walked away as if nothing had occurred.

To Be Continued...

Also available by Blake Karrington

Country Boy
Country Boy 2
Trapstar
Country Boy 3

Coming Soon

Trapstar 2

Made in the USA
Monee, IL
05 November 2022

17201190R00114